Medicine Goes Corporate:

My Tale of Corruption, Injustice, and Greed

By

Jack Spenser, M.D.

ISBN: 979-8-218-08334-2

Medicine Goes Corporate: My Tale of Corruption, Injustice, and Greed is a work of fiction. Names, characters, places, organizations, and incidents are the product of myth and the author's imagination. Any relationship to actual events, locales, business establishments, organizations, and persons, living or dead, is coincidental.

"Righteous art thou, O Lord,
When I complain to thee;
Yet I would plead my case before thee.
Why does the way of the wicked prosper?
Why do all who are treacherous thrive?
Thou plantest them and they take root;
They grow and they bring forth fruit."

Jeremiah 12: 1–2

PREFACE

MAY 2017

My psychiatrist told me I have to write this book.

I resisted. "I dunno about that. Who would read it?"

She said, "Lots of people."

"I doubt that. Nobody cares about what happened to me."

"But this book isn't about you. It's about injustice."

"Nobody cares about injustice either."

"I disagree. People care about *overcoming injustice*. Hell, that's the plot of over half the movies made today. Tap into that."

We stopped talking. I looked around Dr. Conner's office. Before it became her workplace, it was the library of a two-story white brick mansion built during the 1930s near the historic center of Midwest City. In the 1970s the neighborhood fell into disrepair and stayed there for a few decades. Then, as part of gentrification over the last fifteen years, this stately building was one of many converted into offices for medical professionals. The one I was in was for people working in mental health. Psychiatrists and psychologists had remodeled the living quarters into offices where they could see patients. My doctor ended up in what had been the library on the first floor, closest to the street. It was 4:30 in the afternoon, springtime. Natural light streamed through two double-hung windows and filled the room all the way up to the vaulted ceiling. The room was largely empty. An unoccupied desk occupied one corner opposite the window. The small lamp on the desk surface provided a yellow glow, but little additional light. The two of us were in the other corner opposite the window. A second lamp was on a small table to the left of where I was sitting. Dr. Conner sat across from me.

Dr. Conner continued: "Plus, what happened to you is happening to all doctors. Not just you."

She should know. Her husband is a radiologist. Her daughter is a pediatrician.

Dr. Conner said, "My husband's radiology group just got bought out by a national company, a huge corporation. Now they have all these metrics in place, which are monitored to make sure they are productive, and to make sure that there is no way any of the radiologists is not working hard all the time. He wants to quit. I suggested he just work at his own pace, and when he doesn't meet his quota, well, they can fire him – no big deal. He wants to retire anyway.

"And my daughter, the pediatrician, same thing. When she finished her training, she went to work at her med school, and she has all these quotas in place, like how many patients she has to see in a certain amount of time, which works out to, like, five minutes a patient! That's not enough time. She can't do her job the way it's supposed to be done.

"And me. My days of being a psychiatrist are numbered. Every year there are more and more mandated changes, things I have to do to keep my practice open. Everything is going digital. I can't write prescriptions on a prescription pad anymore; I have to use e-prescribe and use an electronic medical record. God help me if the state comes in and audits me and I show them a bunch of old-fashioned paper charts. I hate technology. It's like learning a second language as an adult, it can be done, but it's hard. These young people, they grew up with this stuff, so it comes natural to them, but not to me.

"And the expense for all this electronic equipment! The only practices that can afford these upgrades are the big practices and the big companies – who want me out of business. The payers, insurance companies, and the government want employee psychiatrists pushing pills – antidepressants, antipsychotics...because it's cheaper than psychiatrists doing psychotherapy. Everything in medicine is going corporate, and no one is telling that story. You need to."

I said, "Sounds like *you* need to write that book."

She shook her head. "These are just petty things. I don't really have any enemies. I never had anyone try to destroy me; I was never important enough for that kind of hate. If someone did to me what Excel and Merciful did to you, I would *have to* write that book."

"I'm scared. Writers who are scared don't write very good books."

"Write it the way you wrote *Diary of a Malpractice Lawsuit*. Keep a diary."

"Back then I wasn't the owner of a business, and I had the time and energy to keep a diary. That's not the case now. Plus, I'm too old, and I just want to be a nobody."

Dr. Conner is very tall, used to play varsity basketball in high school and college. I'm short. Dr. Conner sat up very straight. I looked up. "Well, at least do this," she said. "Keep the paperwork. Keep the records. Then when it's over, use those notes to write the book. Don't do it for me. Don't do it for your readers. Do it for yourself."

A year later, Dr. Connor retired.

This is that book.

PART ONE

1949–2016

CHAPTER 1

This story takes place in Pathfinder, a small town in a Midwestern state with land so flat that giants play croquet on fields of wheat in the summer and have snowball fights in the winter. When I was born here in 1949, Pathfinder was a town of about 20,000 people. It was thirty miles away from the largest city in the state, Midwest City. Going to the big city meant getting on a train or driving through thirty miles of countryside.

Pathfinder was a company town, home of an Amalgamated Meatpacking factory where my dad worked, along with 1,500 other people. Amalgamated Meatpacking Corporation was the largest meatpacking company in the world, converting cattle and hogs to steaks, hamburger, pork chops, and SPAM. The factory was a good employer, paying good union wages. My mom, like most mothers in the 1950s, worked in the home, raising me, my brother, and two sisters.

American corporations like Ford, General Motors, Boeing, and Amalgamated Meatpacking were the pride of the country. They helped win World War II by building tanks and planes. They say an army marches on its stomach, and Amalgamated Meatpacking made the SPAM that fed the troops. After the war, my dad continued to eat SPAM. So did I. So did everyone I knew.

I felt incredibly blessed to live in Pathfinder and the USA. The depression was over. World War II was won. Our country had incredible resources – coal, oil, water, and the fertile Midwest farmland, where we grew the crops that fed the world.

In the Pathfinder Public School System, I was taught that our country had a good government, fair and democratic. In seventh grade I took a social studies class that described the three branches of government in Washington, DC, which was described in hushed tones as hallowed ground, where the legislative branch passed the laws, the judicial branch made sure the laws were just, and the executive branch enforced the law. It was emphasized that we had a democratic government because our representatives and senators were voted into office by fair elections. So was the president. It was our responsibility as citizens to vote. Politicians were held in high esteem. When I was a young boy, I met one of our senators at the Midwest City airport, and everyone treated him like a hero. I was impressed by his firm handshake.

Nothing was emphasized more in that social studies class than freedom of speech. You could be the chief executive officer of the Amalgamated Meatpacking factory, or a worker on the production line, or the president of the Pathfinder Bank, or a teacher, or a farmer, or a laborer – it made no difference: you had a right to express your thoughts and beliefs about anything. This was best illustrated by the famous Norman Rockwell painting on the cover of the *Saturday Evening Post* in 1943. It illustrates a town hall meeting where a workingman, dressed in workingman attire, stands and speaks. And everyone listens, including those dressed in coats and ties. This illustration, to me, was not only a message of freedom of speech, but a message of fairness, that government treated everyone equally. The rich and connected could not take advantage of those with lesser means. There was freedom of opportunity. That was drilled into us from every corner – parents, school, church, and the media of the time – radio and television.

Disagreements were okay. Debate was good. In my social studies textbook there was a black-and-white photograph of several men and women sitting on the front porch, enjoying a summer evening and discussing the issues of the day. "This is democracy," said the caption.

There was economic freedom as well. The Main Street of Pathfinder was lined by small shops and businesses – clothing stores, dentist offices, insurance agencies, barber shops, grocery stores, restaurants, and the offices of the daily newspaper, the *Pathfinder Guide and Tribune*. A person could prosper by going to work at a big corporation like Amalgamated Meatpacking, but one could also prosper by starting, purchasing, or working at a small business – a radio/TV shop, office supply company, plumbing company, or hardware store. One could also work as a professional and make a good living as a lawyer, accountant, dentist, or physician – working independently as a sole practitioner or with a partner or two.

I recognize that looking back at my childhood from adulthood is like looking through tinted glasses, and things could not have been as rosy as I remember them. Nevertheless here is the way I saw Pathfinder and Midwest State as I grew up: There was general prosperity, a sense of everyone working together, without extremes of rich and poor. The rich were rich, but not that much richer than the rest of us, and no one begrudged the money the well-off earned because they were CEOs or professionals with a lot of responsibility who had to work hard. There was a sense of fairness and community. My father worked on the factory line of Amalgamated Meatpacking, but I played on the same Little League baseball team as the son of the Amalgamated CEO. We went swimming at the same municipal swimming pool. We attended the same public schools – along with the daughter of the bank president, the kids of all the owners of the small businesses in town, and their employees. That wasn't remarkable because the public school system was the only school choice in the community. For private schooling a kid had to go to a boarding school. No one I knew went to boarding school.

This was the Zeitgeist of my youth – liberty, freedom, and equality.

As I got older, Pathfinder grew, and Midwest City grew, and the town and city kept getting closer together. Finally, when I left home to go to college, there was no clear demarcation between the two. The countryside had been replaced by subdivisions and shopping malls so that Pathfinder imperceptibly merged into Midwest City. Thus, Pathfinder was a suburb of Midwest City for better or worse.

I went to college at Midwest State University, where I majored in chemistry. I was also a varsity wrestler, at 133 pounds. I went through college in three years. I was a man in a hurry.

When I graduated from college, I went to Midwest State University Medical School and graduated from there in 1974. Then I did four years of a pathology residency at the same institution. When I finally finished my training, I went to work as a pathologist at Excel Pinnacle Hospital, the only hospital in Pathfinder. I worked there for the next forty-one years.

CHAPTER 2

February 2014

Excel Pinnacle Hospital was a typical suburban hospital. It was eight stories tall, towering above the flat Midwestern plains. It was the tallest building in Pathfinder, a beacon of good medical care. It had everything the community needed for its healthcare wants – 220 hospital beds, 8 operating rooms, and ancillary services that were state of the art. The hospital was owned by Excel Hospital Corporation, the nation's largest hospital company with more than three hundred healthcare facilities and about 275,000 employees. Excel Corp built an eight-story medical office building across the street from Excel Pinnacle Hospital, and most of the doctors on the medical staff had their offices there. At the level of the sixth floor, the two buildings were connected by a walkway that extended over the road so that the pediatricians, surgeons, internists, pulmonologists, and other specialists could take the walkway to the hospital and easily check on their inpatients at the hospital – a good way to keep the medical staff happy, close by, and locked into the hospital.

At Excel Pinnacle Hospital we had a good thing going. Everyone knew their place. Therefore, the hospital was well prepared for Rob Sorley when he came to the emergency room with belly pain. Rob was a good old boy who worked for a trucking company, which provided good health insurance from the Merciful Insurance Company. However, Rob didn't use his insurance much. He didn't believe in doctors, who, he thought, overestimated what they could do. So Rob endured the abdominal pain, which got pretty bad and then went away and then came back worse than ever. He became so weak that he couldn't walk. His wife brought him to our Excel Pinnacle emergency room. It was a Saturday afternoon, in the dead of winter, but Rob couldn't wait. He was dying.

Rob Sorley received excellent care. Within five minutes of arriving at the hospital, an emergency room physician, Dr. Frank Moneypenny, examined the patient. The exam didn't take long. Dr. Moneypenny put his hand on McBurney's point in the right lower quadrant of the abdomen and gently pressed inward. Rob almost jumped to the ceiling in pain. Dr. Moneypenny strongly suspected a diagnosis of ruptured acute appendicitis, with sepsis. An ER nurse started an IV line in the patient, and Dr. Moneypenny ordered normal saline infused as rapidly as possible. He then sent the patient straight to the radiology department for a stat CT scan. He also phoned Dr. Anderson Spickard, the general surgeon on call, who made it to the hospital in thirty minutes. By that time the results of the CT scan confirmed the diagnosis of ruptured acute appendicitis, a serious disease, and Rob was on his way to the operating room.

At the OR, Dr. Spickard was waiting, anxious to start the emergency appendectomy. Less than an hour had passed since Rob first came to the emergency room.

During the operation, Dr. Spickard found that, in fact, the appendix had ruptured, and thus the contents of the appendix were in the abdominal cavity, where they didn't belong – especially since bacteria were along for the ride. The result was a life-threatening infection. Rob Sorley's body did its best to limit the damage: fat in the abdomen migrated to the region of the appendix and sealed off the area. White blood cells rushed to the site to combat the bacteria. Nevertheless, it was a losing battle unless the cause of the problem, the ruptured appendix, was removed.

That's what Dr. Spickard did. He took out the source of the problem, the ruptured appendix. Then he washed out the area with copious amounts of normal saline. He cauterized or tied off anything that was bleeding, leaving a nice clean abdomen. Then he fixed everything that was damaged. He started by repairing the defect the removed appendix left, and finished by tying together the two edges of the skin incision with stitches that he sewed delicately, like a seamstress repairing a torn garment.

During the operation and for ten days after the operation, Mr. Sorley received an intravenous cocktail of antibiotics – ampicillin, clindamycin, and gentamicin – because there were a lot of bacteria in the abdomen and bloodstream that needed killing.

After the operation Rob went to the recovery room and then his room. For the next few days a hospitalist, Dr. Ted Fresca, took care of him, making sure the antibiotics were continued, and that he had the correct amount of IV fluids to keep him out of shock, but not too much fluid to overload his heart. Dr. Fresca also gave Rob medicines that he needed to be comfortable and on the road to recovery.

While the patient was in the hospital, I examined the appendix that Dr. Spickard removed. That was my job as a pathologist, to study disease, specifically what disease processes were present in the appendix, if any. The appendix I received from the operating room was immersed in formalin, a fixative that kept the tissues preserved from Saturday afternoon when the operation was done, to Monday morning when I did the "gross examination" of the specimen, i.e., inspected it using my two good eyes, and dissected it using my instruments – scissors, scalpel, forceps, and anything else I needed to get the job done.

I was impressed with the specimen. The relatively large appendix had a perforation in its wall about the size of two pencil tips, not much, but big enough to let bacteria leak out into the abdominal cavity, where it caused all kinds of problems, including life-threatening sepsis. I dictated my observations using a hands-free dictating machine. Using my tools, I took representative tissue samples of the appendix and put them into cassettes, small plastic holders with perforations to let in chemicals. A few miles away from the hospital I owned a laboratory with equipment, processors, and chemicals. Trained laboratory workers called histotechnologists worked overnight to process, cut, and stain Mr. Sorley's appendix tissue. The end result was a thin piece of stained tissue on a glass slide that I could examine with my microscope.

My company, Pathology Services, had the contract with Excel Pinnacle to do the pathology work for the hospital. Pathology Services had always had this contract since the hospital was built in 1973, when I was still in medical school. When I returned to Pathfinder after my medical training, I went to work at Pathology Services; then after some years when I purchased Pathology Services, I was continuing a long tradition.

And part of that tradition was me, a pathologist, looking at Rob Sorley's appendix with my microscope. I confirmed the diagnosis of acute appendicitis with rupture, but there was something else there as well. I saw a malignant tumor, with the long complicated name of low-grade mucinous cystadenocarcinoma. It wasn't all bad – "low grade" was better than "high grade," but the tumor was still malignant and could kill Mr. Sorley just as well as a high-grade tumor, albeit a bit slower.

I dictated my findings, which were typed up by one of our four transcriptionists, who were also employees of Pathology Services. My report went to Rob Sorley's medical chart, with copies to Dr. Spickard, Dr. Fresca, and any other doctor who took care of the patient. I also phoned Dr. Spickard and told him my findings. I told Dr. Spickard what I'd mentioned in my report, that the appendix had a low-grade cancer, and that this cancer went to the surgical margins of the specimen – thus it had been incompletely removed. Dr. Spickard had more work to do.

The next day Dr. Spickard took Rob back to the operating room, where he removed the rest of the malignant tumor. When the operation was over, Mr. Sorley went to the recovery room and then his patient room.

Once again Dr. Fresca took care of Mr. Sorley while he recovered from this second operation.

I examined this second surgical specimen. I found some residual tumor in the specimen, but this "leftover" cancer had been completely removed. The lymph nodes did not have any tumor, so there were no metastases. It was a good report. Mr. Sorley was cured.

The only thing left to do was send out the bills:

Dr. Moneypenny, the emergency room doctor, sent a bill to the Merciful Insurance Company for the services he performed, payable to Emergency Physicians' Services, PC, a company he owned with his partner Dr. Doug Smith.

Dr. Spickard sent a bill to Merciful for his professional surgical services, including the two operations.

Dr. Fresca sent Merciful a bill for taking care of the patient in the hospital. This was payable to the hospital services company he worked for.

Finally, I sent a bill to Merciful on behalf of my company, Pathology Services, PC. Actually, I sent two bills:

1. A bill for the physician/pathologist services I performed when I looked at the two specimens and rendered my diagnoses and interpretations. Picture a doctor/ pathologist looking through a microscope at slides of a patient's specimen and making diagnoses and interpretations. That's what I did, and my company sent a bill for that.

2. An additional bill for the costs of preparing the microscopic slides I looked at. Picture a laboratory in a building with laboratory equipment, processors, and chemicals where lab workers in white coats make microscopic slides of tissue for a pathologist to look at. It's like a methamphetamine lab. But instead of making an illegal drug, it makes microscopic slides for pathologists to examine and interpret. To cover those pathology lab costs, my company sent a bill.

It was a great deal for everyone. The patient got good care with little to no cost, because Merciful Insurance Company paid most or all of the medical bills from premiums paid predominantly or entirely by the patient's employer. The hospital got paid and made a profit. The physicians got paid and made a good living. And Merciful Insurance Company did well too. Real well. Even after paying all these medical bills, Merciful had enough money left over from premiums to meet a hefty payroll and put billions of dollars of reserves in the bank. Everyone worked together, and everyone profited.

Then it all fell apart.

CHAPTER 3

Our healthcare system is like a coral reef, which survives because every living being populating the reef has a function, and everything is in balance. The hard coral provides structure and a protected environment where algae can live. In return the algae provide oxygen and carbohydrates, which enable the coral to survive. The living coral secretes calcium carbonate to make a limestone habitat for small fish, lobsters, eels, and crabs. These smaller fish and creatures are food for the larger fish – groupers, barracudas, and sharks. Parrot fish eat algae and secrete sand. The sandy bottom is used as a habitat for flounders and jawfish that hide in the sand and poke their heads out to eat plankton. And so on. The end result is a functioning living coral reef, one of the most beautiful creations in existence. But everything has to be in balance.

I hope I demonstrated in the previous chapter that the healthcare ecosystem has a similar makeup. There is the backbone, the hospital building itself. Then there are the creatures, I mean people, who populate this structure – the ER docs, radiologists, surgeons, hospitalists, and pathologists who work together, along with nurses, operating room staff, technologists, housekeeping personnel, pharmacists, anesthesiologists and anesthetists...the list is a long one, almost endless. A hospital is as complex as a coral reef. Every department depends on the other departments to be competent and to do their jobs. And the sustenance that keeps everything running is money, which in today's healthcare system comes largely from insurance companies and the government.

An ecosystem like a reef, or a healthcare system, is a fragile thing, really. You can't just have sharks or only coral or one species of fish – even pretty clown fish. You need it all; you need balance. One change, even a minor one, can have huge consequences. For example, lionfish, native to the Pacific Ocean, were accidentally introduced into the Caribbean Sea, with catastrophic consequences. The enemies that lionfish have in the Pacific are absent in the Caribbean. Therefore, the lionfish population in the Caribbean has exploded. Lionfish are very successful eaters of small fish, too successful, actually. If the small fish disappear, the large fish disappear. And there are other side effects. The lionfish eat too many of the parrot fish, which eat the algae, so the algae builds up. No longer is the water around the reef crystal clear, but a cloudy green. The excess algae can choke the reef to death. One seemingly minor change, an excess population of one fish species, can threaten the existence of the entire reef.

A healthcare system is similar. Every part has to work in symbiosis – the patients, hospitals, doctors, nurses, ancillary services, insurance companies, government payers...everyone. When that happened, and for many decades it *did* happen, the result was the best healthcare system in the world. However, over the last ten to twenty years, healthcare has gone corporate. Consolidation has happened; bigger is thought to be better. The big fish are eating the small fish, and the healthcare ecosystem is out of balance. And it's dying. So are patients.

CHAPTER 4

The wrongdoing went on for years and affected doctors and patients. The doctors in this story are not particularly sympathetic victims because, for the most part, doctors live a good life, and no one feels sorry for doctors. Nevertheless, many of the doctors in this story were unlucky enough to lose their livelihood. I was one of them.

Of course, the sympathetic victims in this story are the patients. As a physician, I am telling this story from the viewpoint of a physician. Nevertheless, as you read what the insurance companies and hospital corporations did to doctors, be aware that what affected physicians also affected patients. But of course you knew that, dear reader. You are one of them.

CHAPTER 5

1983–2015

They went after the emergency room docs first. The Emergency Room Department was the strongest department in Excel Pinnacle Hospital, because of Dr. Frank Moneypenny and Dr. Doug Smith. They owned the practice that provided the ER docs to the hospital's emergency room.

Doug and Frank had a long history with Excel Pinnacle Hospital, almost as long as I did. They both started working in the Excel Pinnacle emergency room in 1983, a little after I started. They were fresh out of their residency training and eager to change the world. For the first few years they worked as employees of an older physician, Claude McDermott, who had the contract to provide ER docs to the hospital.

Doug and Frank came to their positions with board certification in emergency room medicine. Most ER docs in the early 1980s were not board certified. Emergency room medicine was just getting started as a specialty, and emergency rooms were staffed by a potpourri of physicians with variable training and competence. Some were older semi-retired physicians, like Claude McDermott. Others were young doctors in training who moonlighted while they were doing their internships, residencies, or fellowships. Some found that they liked working in the ER better than working as an intern or resident. In some ways training could be a real hassle – a lot of work for little pay. Moonlighting in the ER was relatively little work for a lot of pay. So one common pathway to a career in emergency room medicine was to terminate a residency in internal medicine or surgery or some other specialty and then go to work covering shifts in the emergency room.

There weren't really any standards at the time, and pretty much anyone with a medical license could call himself or herself an ER doctor. The field attracted some good doctors, but some marginal ones as well, those who couldn't make it in any of the other specialties. Some ER docs were just marking time until they went into some other specialty or retired. But in the early 1980s, emergency room medicine started to become established as a real specialty with training requirements, tests for competence, and a pathway for board certification – just like internal medicine, general surgery, pathology, and the other medical specialties.

When Doug and Frank started working at the Excel Pinnacle ER in 1983, they were the only two physicians in Claude McDermott's group who were board certified in ER medicine. This state of affairs continued until 1989 when the hospital asked Dr. McDermott's group to provide only board-certified ER physicians to work in the emergency room. Dr. McDermott said that was impossible.

After this negative response, the Excel Pinnacle administration asked Frank Moneypenny and Doug Smith to submit a proposal, which they did, and it was accepted. Dr. McDermott retired, and Drs. Moneypenny and Smith took over the emergency room contract. They established a group/company called Emergency Physician Services, PC.

The newly constituted group started out with three physicians – Frank, Doug, and one physician employee. All three were board certified in emergency room medicine, the first group in the state to be composed entirely of certified ER docs. Since there were only three of them, each had to work long hours to keep the emergency room staffed – every month each of the physicians worked twenty to twenty-one shifts of twelve hours each – long exhausting days.

But they did it. Over the next twenty-six years, Emergency Physician Services, PC, grew to nineteen physicians. The group had to grow because the hospital grew. The ER went from 19,000 annual visits to 50,000 visits. The quality did not suffer with the growth, however. In fact, it continued to improve. The Excel Pinnacle emergency room was the first in the state to convert to all dictated reports for all patient encounters. They continued to be the only ER group in the state composed 100% of board-certified emergency room doctors. There were never any adverse medical malpractice judgments or settlements against any of their ER docs – not one. Simply put, they were the strongest department in the hospital.

Then the hospital got greedy.

I found out what happened late on a Friday afternoon in June 2015. I was sitting in my office, wrapping up the week. My office is small and simple. My chair is a working chair with a back but no arms so that my arms are free to work. I sit facing the only door at a small L-shaped desk, which sits against one wall. An AO 110 microscope sits on the short leg of the L. The main part of my desk is usually empty. I have a one-touch rule – a document comes into my office, I touch it and deal with it – sign it, pass it on to the next person, file it, or throw it away – do whatever it takes to get the document off my desk. The wall behind where I sit is covered by floor-to-ceiling bookshelves filled with textbooks about pathology and medicine. The wall on the other side of my desk is beige and empty, and in the small space between that wall and my desk sits a chair that is available for any visitors to use. To my left are file cabinets, where I keep copies of scientific and medical articles.

On that late Friday afternoon, Dr. Frank Moneypenny came into my office to talk. Frank is a tall lanky angular guy. Everything about his anatomy is sharp – sharp elbows, knees, ankles, feet, nose – no fat on him, and on top he has a mat of dark hair. Frank kind of loped into my office, quickly sat down in the chair on the other side of my desk, and slumped down.

"We just got fired," he said.

"Huh?" I intelligently replied.

Frank just sat there, too upset to talk.

After a long enough pause, I said, "What happened?"

"Bart Magnum fired us. He's giving the ER contract to a company called Benevolent Holdings."

I knew who Bart Magnum was. Everyone at the hospital knew who Bart Magnum was. He was the chief executive officer of the hospital.

I said, "Benevolent Holdings? Never heard of them."

"It's a large national company that provides physicians to hospitals. The hospital ER is going corporate."

What do you say in a situation like this? I tried this: "I'm really sorry. It's not right."

"Yeah."

"You know there is not a damn thing I can do about it, right?"

"I know. I just wanted you to hear about it from me."

"So what are you going to do? Stay on, maybe work with the new company – what was it?"

"Benevolent Holdings."

"Got it."

"Not going to happen. Magnum fired me and Doug. Everyone else in the department can stay on and work for the new group except me and Doug. Magnum wants us gone. He said he was quite happy to fire us – that he was tired of 'putting up with our crap,' as he put it."

I wasn't surprised. Frank and Doug were never ones to keep their thoughts to themselves. From their standpoints, if something in the ER or the hospital needed correcting, they would point it out regardless of whose feelings were hurt. If that meant some people, including Bart Magnum, got their feelings hurt or needed to change their ways, so be it.

Frank continued, "The other reason I came here is to give you a heads-up. Watch your back. Benevolent Holdings not only provides ER docs, but provides other hospital-based services, including pathology. You may be next."

"Thanks for the warning."

"You're good at what you do, Jack. Everyone knows that. But I'm here to tell you being good isn't enough to keep your job."

I nodded. He walked out.

Over the next few weeks, the reason for the change from Emergency Physician's Services, PC, to Benevolent Holdings became clear. Of course the reason was money. Benevolent Holdings was 50% owned by Excel Hospital Corporation. Thus, the change in vendors from Emergency Physician Services, PC, to Benevolent Holdings increased the profits of Excel Hospital Corp in at least three ways:

1. Since Benevolent was 50% owned by Excel, the profits for ER physician services were divided up this way: half for Benevolent and half for Excel. Whereas previously all emergency room physician reimbursement went to Emergency Physicians Services, now 50% went to Excel Corp. It was like manna from heaven.

2. Frank and Doug lost their jobs, which lowered expenses and increased profits for Benevolent/Excel Corp. Nothing like this good old-fashioned method of eliminating jobs to decrease the payroll and increase profits. Not only that but payroll costs decreased in another way: The ER physicians employed by Frank and Doug were offered a choice by Benevolent and Excel Pinnacle – they could keep the jobs they had at half the pay they had been getting, or they could resign. Those who resigned were quickly replaced by physicians already employed by Benevolent, who were paid half as much money as the doctors they replaced – another great way to increase profits for Benevolent and Excel.

Note: the reimbursements from the insurance companies (United, Cigna, Medicare, Medicaid, Blue Cross/Blue shield, Merciful, and others) stayed the same. However, instead of that money going to the owners and doctors of Emergency Physician Services, PC, the money went to Benevolent Holdings, which passed on half of it to Excel Corp. What a good deal for Excel Corp! Before the change, Excel Pinnacle received NO INCOME from staffing the ER with doctors – all the revenues and profits went to the doctors doing the work. But after the switch to Benevolent Holdings, half the profits went to Excel Corp. Those profits were quite substantial because the payroll costs had decreased so much.

3. Then there was the lagniappe. The new batch of emergency room docs were essentially employees of Excel Pinnacle Hospital, since Excel owned 50% of Benevolent, the

company signing their paychecks. Therefore, various subtle and not so subtle measures were instituted to make sure that these doctor employees did all they could to make things lucrative for Excel Pinnacle Hospital. New "metrics" were applied to the emergency room physicians. Some were reasonable, perhaps. For example, the number of patients a doctor took care of during a shift was monitored, and there were quotas – like four patients an hour to make sure the ER docs were working and not loafing. Nothing wrong with that, I guess – measures of productivity are certainly in place in other industries – warehouse and assembly line workers certainly have such metrics.

But some of the metrics were not ethical, in my opinion. For example, how many patients each ER doc admitted to Excel Pinnacle Hospital was tracked, and the more patients a doctor admitted to the hospital, the better – the more patients admitted, the higher revenues to the hospital. There was pressure to make sure that a certain relatively high percentage of patients examined by the doctors in the ER was admitted to the hospital for further workup and treatment – especially if the patients admitted had good insurance and could pay their hospital bills. A good way for an ER physician to do well on his or her evaluations, and get a good bonus, was to admit as many patients to the hospital as possible. Call me naive, but I think whether a patient is admitted to the hospital or not should solely depend on the medical condition of the patient, not whether the hospital had beds to fill by well-paying patients.

So it was all good for Excel. There had to be a catch though, right?

There was. The quality of care given in the emergency room went down, a lot. That wasn't too surprising. The doctors employed by Benevolent at half the pay of their predecessors were half as good, if that. Sadly, what had been the strongest department in the hospital, the emergency room, turned into the weakest.

The other physicians on the Excel Pinnacle medical staff noticed the decrease in quality of patient care in the ER, and they complained, a lot. These complaints were voiced at the various department meetings of the hospital medical staff – surgery, internal medicine, pediatrics, ob-gyn, and so on.

The problems in the emergency room were also brought up at the monthly executive committee meetings, which included the leaders of the medical staff, and at the quarterly general medical staff meetings, which included everyone on the Excel Pinnacle medical staff. During these meetings physicians wailed and gnashed their teeth and said this change "could not stand."

At these meetings Bart Magnum and the other executives at Excel Pinnacle swore they would look into these issues and "solve any problems they found by getting to the root causes and making the needed changes." Bart said, "Any specific patient incidents you can relate to me would be helpful so that I can find out what happened and use the adverse outcome as a chance for learning and quality improvement." Bart got to listen to descriptions of several such "adverse outcomes."

The following interchange at the monthly ob-gyn meeting was typical. Since I had so many interactions with the ob-gyn department, I was at the meeting representing the pathology department and hospital laboratory.

The ob-gyn meeting took place in a small classroom with tiered seating, a total of three tiers. I sat in the back. I knew there were problems between the ER and the ob-gyn department and the hospital administration, and that there would be fights. So I sat in the back, where I wouldn't get killed in the crossfire.

Bart Magnum was seated in the front row. Rob Masterson, one of the ob-gyn docs, and the chairman of the Ob-Gyn Department, sat in front of the classroom, white dry-erase boards behind him. Rob was a little guy with blond hair, quite high strung. Really high strung. He was literally manic-depressive, although well controlled with his lithium medication. When he got upset, his hands shook. They were shaking as he told this story:

"My patient was a nineteen-year-old woman, a student at the local community college, who came to the ER last Saturday with lower abdominal pain. The doctor who saw her made a diagnosis of pelvic inflammatory disease and sent her home with antibiotics, with instructions to follow up with her ob-gyn doctor, who by the way was me. But no one in the emergency room let me know she was there. The ER doc didn't have the courtesy to phone me and tell me what was going on with my patient – no communication whatsoever! The patient never followed up with me on Monday because she died the next day, Sunday, from hemorrhagic shock caused by a ruptured ectopic pregnancy! She didn't have pain from pelvic inflammatory disease. The pain was caused by an ectopic pregnancy in her right fallopian tube. If the correct diagnosis was made, and I was called in, I could have done an operation to remove the ectopic pregnancy before it ruptured, and the patient would still be alive.

"I hardly know where to begin," Rob continued. "First, the ER doc should have phoned me to tell me what was going on. Second, a pregnancy test should have been done – didn't happen. Third, even without doing those things, a correct diagnosis of an ectopic pregnancy should have been suspected or at least considered."

While Rob was telling this sordid tale, Bart Magnum listened and took notes on a yellow legal pad. He looked like a typical hospital administrator for Excel Corp, and I've met dozens. I think they are made by a cookie cutter labeled "corporate Twinkie." He was a little over six feet tall, slim, with dark hair nicely parted on the left and combed to the right. He was dressed in a dark suit with a white shirt and solid red tie. He was handsome in a sleazy kind of way. When Rob had finished, Bart shook his head sadly. He said, "Well, we will certainly investigate this incident thoroughly and make sure something like this doesn't happen again." He asked Rob for the name of the patient and the exact date and time all this happened.

It was Rob's turn to shake his head. He said, "There's not a damn thing you're going to do about it, which means there's not a damn thing I can do about it."

Bart said, "I'll look into this and get back with you with some answers."

Rob said, "I doubt that."

Rob was right. There was no follow-up. Bart didn't care a thing about what Rob Masterson thought, or, for that matter, what any of the doctors thought. I mean, what were the doctors going to do? Go to another hospital? The others were just as bad, so that wasn't going to happen. And even if Rob or some of the other docs left Excel Pinnacle for greener pastures elsewhere, Bart would just recruit more doctors to replace them. To Bart and Excel Corp, doctors were all the same, a commodity and replaceable.

There were other problems with the changes in the emergency room. The Benevolent ER docs admitted more patients to the hospital than their predecessors, a lot more patients, probably too many patients. The system broke down. So many patients were admitted that sometimes no hospital beds were available. Patients had to wait in "holding areas" or in the emergency room itself while they waited for a bed to be available. Twelve-to-twenty-four-hour waits occurred. Bart Magnum and Excel Pinnacle Hospital were delighted. Revenues were up.

Patients did not share in their joy, however. And neither did the surgeons, internists, gynecologists, and other members of the medical staff who had to reckon with an emergency room staffed by substandard physicians.

And that is the story of how the Emergency Room Department went from the strongest department in the hospital to the weakest.

And I did nothing, because I can assure you with 100% certainty that absolutely nobody cared what I thought.

CHAPTER 6

2014–2016

The hospitalists were the next group of doctors to be terminated without cause by Excel Pinnacle.

After the downfall of the ER department, the strongest department of the hospital was composed of the hospitalists, who were the doctors who took care of patients while they were in the hospital. But only when the patients were in the hospital. Once the patients were discharged from the hospital, they went back to the care of their regular docs.

The hospitalists were employed by the Newcombe Medical Group founded by Dr. Bob Newcombe, who was a renaissance man. Not only was he an excellent physician, an internist, but he was that rarity in medicine — a well-rounded person who was smart about things other than science and medicine — like literature, art, other cultures...Most doctors aren't. They are ignorant of anything outside of their specialty. It makes me weep. In his spare time, Bob got a fine arts degree from Ivory University in nearby Midwest City; he invited me to his graduation. He was a mentor to me.

Dr. Newcombe was also a good businessman and CEO of his company, Newcombe Medical Group, PC, a group of ten internal medicine doctors. Newcombe Medical Group had their offices in the building across the street from Excel Pinnacle Hospital and admitted patients to that hospital.

Newcombe Medical Group also had the contract to provide hospitalist physicians to Excel Pinnacle Hospital. So, since Dr. Newcombe was essentially in charge of the hospitalist program, he was the individual who hired and fired the hospitalists on the Excel

Pinnacle medical staff. Dr. Newcombe had high standards, and thus only top-notch board-certified physicians were hired and kept on.

Dr. Newcombe assigned one of those doctors, Dr. Ted Fresca, to be the chairman of the Hospitalist Department. Dr. Fresca was an excellent well-trained physician who went to medical school and did his training at nearby Ivory Medical School in Midwest City. He not only took care of the hospitalist department, but also stepped up and provided leadership for the entire medical staff.

For example, when Excel Pinnacle Hospital decided to switch from paper medical records to an electronic medical record system (EMR), Dr. Fresca headed up the steering committee that made the transition. His hospitalist department did the pilot study of the new EMR for the entire Excel Corporation and helped correct the bugs and flaws. When the improved EMR was finally ready to go live, Dr. Fresca set up the training program to teach the other members of the medical staff how to use it – the surgeons, internists, radiologists, pathologists...everyone. It was quite an undertaking, involving educational handouts, lectures, and hands-on learning at the computer. This changeover from paper medical records to electronic medical records was successfully, seamlessly done in spite of the fact that the medical staff was populated by conservative, change-resistant technophobes.

I was one of those conservative change-resistant technophobes. It took me a whole day to learn the new system. Ted Fresca was my teacher, patiently going over how to look up the history of the patient and the physical findings, and where to find the X-ray results and all the other information I needed. He showed me how to record the operative note when I did a bone marrow aspiration and biopsy, and how to write the post-op orders. Ted was a good teacher, and we got the learning session done in spite of frequent interruptions from other pupils and teachers needing help. Ted looked very tired and stressed, but never lost his cool.

The changeover to the EMR was completed ahead of schedule, with no problems, largely due to the indispensable help of Dr. Fresca and his staff of hospitalist colleagues.

Dr. Ted Fresca was promptly fired. So were all the hospitalists.

Again, I found out about it in my office. On a late Thursday afternoon in the fall of 2016, Dr. Ted Fresca came to see me. Ted was a big guy, a bear of a man, who looked like a linebacker for the Chicago Bears. Actually though, he was more of a teddy bear than a real bear, who had a gentle countenance and manner. He sat down in my office. He looked relaxed and about ten years younger than the last time I saw him, which had been at my training session for the EMR. He sat at the chair on the other side of my desk from me and asked, "Do you have a few minutes?"

"Of course," I said.

"Tomorrow is my last day."

"Why?"

"Excel Pinnacle is cancelling our contract. Bart Magnum told this to Dr. Newcombe earlier in the week, who passed on the news to me. Needless to say, Dr. Newcombe is ticked off about it."

That stopped me. After a pause I said, "So am I. You had a strong department, one of the strongest in the hospital."

"That's not good enough, I guess. I think they would have gotten rid of us some time ago, except they needed our help to make the electronic medical record work. "

"Did Magnum give you any recognition for all the work you did converting to the EMR – a bonus, a plaque, anything at all?"

"No. Just a termination letter. In fact, everyone in our department was fired, every last one of us."

"That's cold."

"I'm okay, Jack. Actually, I'm in a better place now."

Excel Pinnacle Hospital awarded the hospitalist contract to...you guessed it...Benevolent Holdings. Building on the "success" of the changes in the emergency room, Excel Pinnacle Hospital replaced Dr. Fresca and the rest of Dr. Newcombe's hospitalists with physicians employed by Benevolent Corp, who were paid half as much money. So the end result was that money that previously went to Dr. Newcombe and his hospitalists now went to Benevolent Holdings, with a 50% cut to Excel Corp, which, you recall, owned 50% of Benevolent Holdings.

Talk about a great business decision! Was that great management or what?!

Of course, there was a downside. The new hospitalists hired for half the money tended to be poorly trained and marginally competent, if not incompetent. Patient care suffered because the hospitalists didn't know enough to provide good medical care.

But even worse than that, sometimes patients went long periods of time without being seen or examined by a doctor at all, competent or otherwise, because so few hospitalists were on the job. Beneficial applied the latest in modern management techniques by using "metrics" to schedule the "optimum number" of hospitalists for any given work shift. These "metrics" were supposed to efficiently match the number of working doctors to the workload, with resultant greater productivity of the workforce, i.e., the doctors. Unfortunately, the results on the ground, in the hospital, were a disaster. There were too few hospitalists available to cover the needs of the number of inpatients. The hospitalists weren't productive enough to do what they needed to do. They simply didn't have the time to take care of their patients. Patients died unattended and uncared for, sometimes without being examined by a hospitalist. Hell, they weren't even *seen* by a hospitalist. Diagnoses were not made because there were no doctors available to order the needed tests and studies, and to interpret them. Doses of medicines were missed because the hospitalists didn't get around to ordering them. The quality of hospital inpatient care went down, a lot.

How did I know all this? Well, of course, unofficially I heard various horror stories of poor patient care. Bad news in a hospital travels fast.

In addition, officially, I became aware of various adverse outcomes for patients because I served on the Quality Assurance (QA) Committee. The QA Committee was composed of the chairmen of each of the departments in the hospital – internal medicine, general surgery, ob-gyn, pediatrics, and so on. A total of about fifteen physicians attended the meetings. I attended the meetings because I was the chairman of the pathology department. Bart Magnum and some other corporate Twinkies also attended. We met in a relatively small classroom, with four large white folding tables arranged in a rectangle. The members of the committee sat around the four tables so that we were facing each other. A thick binder was in front of each of the committee members. The binder was filled with the pertinent clinical information of each of the patients to be discussed by the committee. The patients for review were chosen by the physician members of the medical staff, usually because there had been some bad outcome, like a complication or a death. The goal of the committee was to examine the care the patient received, and look for possible areas of improvement to make for better care in the future. However, a pattern developed: the committee reviewed patient record after patient record documenting patients receiving poor medical care in the hospital because of the weaknesses of the new Benevolent hospitalists department.

A short period of time after the change, Dr. Anderson Spickard, a general surgeon, related to the committee the hospital course of one such patient. I and the other members of the committee read the patient information in the binder and followed along while Dr. Spickard highlighted certain parts of the patient's hospital course, which went as follows:

The patient, Ted Oliver, was an obese thirty-one-year-old man who came to the emergency room on a Friday evening, complaining of severe right-upper-quadrant abdominal pain brought on by a big dinner of fried chicken. Dr. Spickard was the surgeon on call. He didn't trust anything the recently hired ER docs said, so he came to the ER and examined the patient himself. Dr. Spickard then ordered the appropriate tests and studies, including a CT scan of the abdomen. He made the diagnosis of acute cholecystitis and decided to operate right away and take out the gallbladder. There was no time to waste. It was a life-threatening situation.

The operation went fine, although the patient was so obese that Dr. Spickard had to do an open cholecystectomy and take out the gallbladder via a relatively large surgical incision. Anderson would have preferred to take out the gallbladder with a laparoscope – simply inserting and using the surgical instruments in a small incision under the guidance of a camera inserted in another small cut. The open cholecystectomy is a relatively major operation, requiring a hospital stay of a few days, and a bigger scar, but that's what Dr. Spickard had to do.

After the operation, Mr. Oliver went to the recovery room. He was a little slow to wake up, but that was probably to be expected from the anesthesia and fairly major surgery. Dr. Spickard dictated an operative note describing what he did. He also did some post-op paperwork. Finally, Dr. Spickard examined his patient in the recovery room; Mr. Oliver was alert enough to answer questions, and his vital signs were good. Dr. Spickard wrote the orders to transfer his patient to a room on the surgical ward, and then went home. It had been a long day and a long week. He hoped the hospitalists could take care of Mr. Oliver during the night.

That didn't happen. When Dr. Spickard made rounds the next afternoon, a Saturday, he found Mr. Spickard comatose. Dr. Spickard ordered a stat blood glucose level and, while that was being done, 50 milliliters of 50% glucose to be given intravenously. The glucose level came back from the lab at 19 mg/dl, a level so low that it was barely compatible with life. The glucose perked up the patient.

Once he was awake, Mr. Oliver informed Dr. Spickard and everyone else taking care of him that he was diabetic, subject to wide swings in his glucose levels, and prone to blackout episodes like this one. Why didn't he tell anyone this ahead of time, before the surgery? No one had asked – not Dr. Spickard, not the ER docs, not the hospitalists...no one.

And here's where it got really bad: not only did the hospitalists not ask about a history of diabetes, the hospitalists didn't ask about anything or check anything – because none of the hospitalists in the hospital that night had any contact with Mr. Oliver whatsoever – no history, no physical examination, no lab work...nothing. There was no evidence that any of the hospitalists even laid eyes on the patient – no admission note, no progress notes...nothing. Dr. Spickard got his patient stabilized over the weekend, and Mr. Oliver went home on Monday, lucky to be alive.

Bart Magnum listened silently and patiently to this sordid tale. When Dr. Spickard completed his summary of the hospital course, Magnum said this: "Thanks to you, I am aware of this incident."

Dr. Spickard said, "That's because after discharging the patient, I came to your office and gave you holy hell."

"Yes, you did. And after you told me about this unfortunate series of events, I immediately phoned the president and CEO of Benevolent. He apologized profusely for the poor care his hospitalists had provided to your patient. I asked him to give you a call, Dr. Spickard, so he could address your concerns directly. Did he call?"

"No."

"Oh...Anyway, his explanation was that the algorithms and metrics Benevolent used said that only two hospitalists were needed per night at a hospital the size of Excel Pinnacle, and that both of the hospitalists on duty that night were too busy taking care of other patients and didn't get around to taking care of Mr. Oliver; instead they were taking care of patients in the Surgical Intensive Care Unit who were going into shock and needed fluids and blood transfusions, as well as patients in the Medical Intensive Care Unit, which was filled up with very sick patients, who had heart problems and were coding without pulse or respiration, which meant the hospitalists had to try to resuscitate them. All that took time, a lot of time. This was an unusual situation. Therefore the hospitalists didn't get around to seeing Mr. Oliver."

Dr. Spickard was not impressed with this explanation. "Sounds like you need to change your algorithms and metrics," he said.

Mr. Magnum said, "I have received assurances from the president of Beneficial himself that this type of unfortunate occurrence will not happen again."

That was the last word at the Quality Assurance meeting.

Nothing changed.

Over the next several months the Quality Assurance Committee continued to meet, and we reviewed similar screw-ups by the hospitalists. Here are a few examples:

1. A patient was admitted with vaginal bleeding. The patient was discharged after receiving transfusions of a few units of blood. Some tissue was admixed with the blood from the vagina, and when I examined the tissue specimen, I saw and reported the presence of early uterine cervical cancer. I phoned the hospitalist who was taking care of the patient, and told him my findings. The hospitalist did

nothing – didn't call in a gynecologist or an oncologist for a consultation, or refer the patient to such a specialist after discharge. Nothing. By the time the patient sought care in Dr. Rob Masterson's office several months later the cancer had metastasized and was incurable.

2. A repeated pattern was that patients on the general medical/surgical floors developed chest pain. The hospitalists tended to diagnose this symptom as anxiety; after all, a hospital is a stressful place. Unfortunately, some of these patients had heart attacks, which went undiagnosed for a while. The lucky ones were eventually admitted to the Medical Intensive Care Unit and treated successfully. Some weren't. Some died.

I could go on and on with similar incidents, but here's the point: patients were suffering and sometimes literally dying, unattended, because the hospitalists were not qualified to provide competent medical care to their patients, or they were unavailable, and the patients received no care whatsoever.

I will give Bart Magnum credit for this. He continued to attend these Quality Assurance Committee meetings. He listened carefully, took notes, and repeatedly made comments like he "would get to the bottom of this" and make sure that Benevolent would "make the needed changes." Then at the follow-up meetings, Bart showed PowerPoint presentations with data that documented the changes Benevolent made to the schedule, to the "algorithms," and to the "metrics," which he promised would solve the problems.

Which didn't happen. These changes didn't help. They were a smokescreen, a way of trying to convince the physicians that what was obviously a problem wasn't really a problem.

Several months after my conversation with Ted Fresca, I had my yearly physical exam, performed by my internist, Dr. Newcombe. After the exam, we talked briefly about the changes at Excel Pinnacle Hospital. Unlike Dr. Fresca, Dr. Newcombe was not "in a better place." He was ticked off that Excel Pinnacle had terminated its contract with him for hospitalist coverage, with the end result that all of the hospitalists Dr. Newcombe had recruited had been fired.

"I don't admit patients there anymore," he said.

"Why?" I asked, even though I knew the answer. I wanted to hear his version of things.

"Because of the low quality of care given to the inpatients," he said. "I'm okay with my patients having same-day surgery there or outpatient treatment, but nothing that requires a hospital stay, even for overnight."

"Have you talked to Bart Magnum about this?"

"Yes."

"Did anything happen for the better?"

"No."

I nodded my head.

Bob continued, "In fact, I've gotten inquiries from his bosses at corporate headquarters, who ask me why I don't support the hospital anymore? I tell them why, and nothing changes."

Losing the support of Dr. Bob Newcombe was a big deal because he had been one of the leaders of the hospital. Dr. Newcombe started his practice about the same time I did, a long time ago, and in the past had been an enthusiastic supporter of the hospital. Like me, Dr. Newcombe had served on the board of the hospital, which was a big honor. Excel Pinnacle had several hundred physicians on staff, but only three physicians at any one time served on the board. Each was elected by the medical staff, so it was a big honor to be elected and serve. Dr. Newcombe was one of the best board members we ever had. He brought his medical training as a physician to the table. However, he had studied subjects other than science and medicine as well. But he wasn't just book smart – he was wise and savvy. Excel Pinnacle Hospital, its physicians, and the patients in the community were well served by Dr. Newcombe. His absence was a big loss to the coral reef that is the healthcare ecosystem.

Finally, the chief of the medical staff, who at the time was Anderson Spickard, lost it.

The venue was the monthly meeting of the Executive Committee of the Hospital. The Executive Committee was composed of the chairmen of each of the various medical staff departments – surgery, internal medicine, pediatrics, ob-gyn, anesthesiology, and radiology...all of them, including me. I was a member of the Executive Committee because I was the chairman of the pathology department. Some of the hospital department heads also attended – the director of Nursing, the director of Quality, the comptroller, and the Operating Room supervisor. Finally, Bart Magnum, the CEO, and David Turner, the chief operating officer, were also there.

There's supposed to be a lot of decorum and good manners at this meeting, which is signaled by the décor. The meetings took place in a large multipurpose room of the hospital, which had been modified to a smaller space by moveable white partitions. White tables were pushed together to form a circle, a symbol of unity. The tables were covered by white tablecloths. The folding chairs had white cushioned seats. Coffee, orange juice and pastries covered a large table in one corner of the room. The table also had sign-in sheets to monitor attendance. These meetings were the best opportunities for the movers and shakers of the hospital to get together to review the past and plan the future of the hospital. The Executive Committee reviewed any and all matters having to do with patient care. It was the most powerful committee of the hospital.

Usually, however, the meetings were boring and uneventful. New capital expenditures were reviewed, along with statistics covering how many admissions occurred the previous month, how many operations were performed, bed occupancy, and similar monotonous information. As part of its oversight duties, the Executive Committee also reviewed the minutes and activities of all the other departments and committees of the hospital. It then approved or did not approve the actions of those bodies. In the past this part of the meeting was as boring as the statistics.

But not this time, when the minutes and activities of the Quality Assurance Committee were reviewed. The poor care of patient after patient, including Dr. Spickard's patient Ted Oliver, was covered in the minutes. The minutes also detailed the sordid details of patients in the hospital not seen, not examined, and not cared for – who suffered complications or even died. It was grim reading.

It also ended the collegial atmosphere of the meeting. When the review was over, Dr. Spickard stood up and shook his head. He was trembling. Dr. Spickard was an athletic-looking man, in his late thirties, movie-star handsome, well over six feet tall, with brown hair. If Central Casting was looking for an actor to play a successful, talented, charismatic surgeon – the search would end with Dr. Anderson Spickard. He had been educated at Loma Linda University Medical School, a Seventh-Day Adventist organization, and Anderson was a Seventh-Day Adventist believer. Thus, he was a vegetarian, without an ounce of fat on him, but quite muscular, and usually easygoing. Not that day. His voice was quavering as he said this: "I don't know what it is going to take to change things, but I have given up. The hospitalists don't show up to take care of our patients, and then if they do, they don't know what they are doing. The situation is so bad that I have told my family and friends not to come to this hospital." Dr. Spickard sat back down.

Bart Magnum, the CEO, stayed seated. In a loud clear voice Bart said this: "Dr. Spickard, I appreciate your candid comments. I can assure you that nothing is more important to me, and to Excel, than patient care. I have taken notes about each of these patient incidents. This performance by the Benevolent hospitalists is unacceptable. I will phone the president of Benevolent, and I will tell him in no uncertain terms that the quality of his hospitalist service has to improve. Our mission at Excel is to provide you and the members of the medical staff the services you need so that all of us can be successful. We will work with you to provide high-quality healthcare to your patients. You have my word on that."

Dr. Spickard said, "I don't believe you."

No one else said anything. Everyone was in shock. In the real world such a confrontation was no big deal. In the setting of a hospital committee meeting, this was a fracture. See, for decades, physicians and healthcare executives worked together to improve patient care. There might be disagreements from time to time on how exactly to do that, but everyone trusted in the good faith of the individuals involved, that everyone had the same goal of good patient care. By the time of this Executive Committee meeting, those days were obviously over.

Bart Magnum said, "Don't go by what I say, go by what I do."

Dr. Spickard shook his head. The meeting was over.

Nothing changed.

I mean that literally. *Nothing* changed. The competence and reliability of the hospitalists remained awful. But Dr. Spickard did not move his practice somewhere else. Instead, he remained on the medical staff at Excel Pinnacle. That was where he sent his patients, and that was where he continued to do his operations. Every other doctor on the medical staff made the same decision. Where else were they going to go? Excel Pinnacle was the only hospital in Pathfinder. The hospitals in Midwest City were a long horrible commute away, and the hospitals there were going through the same pernicious changes as Pathfinder. They were going corporate too.

The hospital business was booming. Excel Pinnacle did not have enough beds to keep up with the number of patients admitted to the hospital. So the hospital built two more floors of patient rooms and added a satellite emergency room facility to handle the increased demand. Six more operating rooms were added. Reimbursements to Excel Pinnacle went up, and with decreased expenses, including the decreased payments to the ER docs and the hospitalists – profits skyrocketed. Excel Pinnacle Hospital was a gold mine.

Which was what Bart Magnum cared about. As an executive at Excel Corp, nothing was more important than meeting his numbers, even if it meant the two strongest departments of the hospital, the ER and the hospitalists, became the weakest. Even if healthcare quality went down. And if he had to face the ire of the physicians of the medical staff and even grovel once in a while, well, the big bucks he earned were worth it.

CHAPTER 7

Why the contrast? Why did it matter to the physicians of the medical staff what kind of care their patients received, but it apparently did not matter to the management of Excel Pinnacle? I'm sure part of it was greed. By scrimping on costs, the Excel Corporation could increase profits, as long as the healthcare quality didn't decrease too much – to the point where there was a scandal or bad publicity. So, part of the contrast was due to different goals: the physicians wanted good care for their patients, and Excel Corp wanted to make as much money as possible.

However, there was another concept involved as well, called "skin in the game." The physicians had it, and the hospital executives did not.

For example, in the case of the emergency room docs, Doug Smith and Frank Moneypenny owned Emergency Physicians Services, PC. With respect to providing good care to the patients coming to the ER, it was their reputations and good names that were on the line. If patient care in the emergency room was suboptimal, then that reflected badly on Doug and Frank. And they cared about their good names. Physicians seem to have an innate need to please, to be thought highly of. They care about what people think. The other doctors on the medical staff knew who the good doctors were, and who the suboptimal doctors were. Heck, everyone who worked at Excel Pinnacle Hospital knew who the good doctors were, and who the not-so-good doctors were. A hospital is a small village, and word gets around. So Doug and Frank did everything they could to keep standards high at Emergency Physician Services and provide good care. They hired and scheduled only qualified well-trained emergency room docs to cover the emergency room twenty-four hours a day, 365 days a year. Finally, to make sure the care rendered at the Excel Pinnacle Hospital ER was topnotch, Doug and Frank worked a lot of the shifts themselves.

Similarly, when Dr. Bob Newcombe owned the group that provided hospitalist physicians to Excel Pinnacle, he wanted the physicians who worked for him to reflect the high standards of his internal medicine group. Everything was connected. If his hospitalists looked bad, then Dr. Newcombe and his group looked bad. He had skin in the game. Therefore, Dr. Newcombe did everything in his power to provide high-quality care to the patients in the hospital. He hired only excellent well-qualified hospitalists; many applied but few were chosen. He terminated the ones who couldn't or wouldn't meet his standards. He scheduled enough hospitalists so that they were enough of them on duty to get the job done right, and gave them the resources they needed to be successful. Also, Dr. Newcombe was often in the hospital himself, checking on his patients and observing the quality of care his hospitalists were providing his patients and the patients of other doctors. If there was a problem, Dr. Newcombe fixed it. He had skin in the game. It was his life.

The executives of Beneficial Corp and Excel Corp didn't have the mentality of Doug Smith, Frank Moneypenny, and Bob Newcombe. They just wanted bodies, minimally paid employees, who would do what they were told with just enough training and experience to work a shift and get by, and hopefully not injure or kill too many patients. And that's what Beneficial and Excel got: the ER docs and hospitalist physicians they employed showed up, put in their time, collected their paychecks, and went home. There was no pride in their work or esprit de corps. It's important to note that the executives of Excel and Beneficial faced no adverse consequences whatsoever for drastically lowering the quality of the ER docs or hospitalists, and the resultant poor patient care. To the contrary, the profits of the hospital went up, and so did their salaries and bonuses.

Bart Magnum and the other executives at Excel and Beneficial didn't have skin in the game. None of them were on the front lines, actually taking care of patients. *They* weren't going to get sued for malpractice or bear any consequences for the resultant poor patient outcomes. How convenient it was to have doctors and nurses as a buffer between the patients and the hospital executives! After all, the Excel and Beneficial Corporate managers weren't healthcare professionals – no, no, no – they didn't have medical licenses or nursing licenses. If a patient wasn't satisfied with his or her care, well, that patient could take it up with his doctor. After all, it was up to the healthcare professionals to provide good medical care, not the bureaucrats.

By keeping costs down, the Excel and Beneficial Corporate executives were able to make their numbers, and nothing was more important to them than making their numbers. By doing so, Bart Magnum and his fellow executives earned their high salaries, bonuses, and raises. Bart Magnum and his fellow corporate executives each made more money than anybody else in the healthcare system, including the doctors, with essentially no liability or responsibilities. What a racket!

CHAPTER 8

2016

To make their numbers, the Excel Pinnacle executives were on a relentless quest to keep costs down. The result was that Excel Pinnacle Hospital purchased the cheapest equipment and supplies available. Unfortunately, "cheap" often meant low quality as well, which didn't matter to Bart Magnum or any of the other executives at Excel Pinnacle Hospital. They didn't have to use any of the stuff they bought. But it sure mattered to those of us trying to take care of sick patients with suboptimal supplies and equipment.

A personal example:

Part of my job was to perform diagnostic bone marrow aspirations and biopsies on patients. The bone marrow is the part of the body where red blood cells, white blood cells, and platelets are made, so looking at the bone marrow can help diagnose what's wrong with a patient, especially a blood disorder like anemia or leukemia. Also, bone marrow is relatively easy to obtain, so it's a good place to look for manifestations of infections or cancer or other diseases.

The easiest, safest place to collect bone marrow is the posterior iliac crest (the back of the hip bone), not the hip joint itself, but the iliac crest, a bulwark of a bone that protects the pelvic structures. It's easily accessible and far away from nerves, large blood vessels, and other things you don't want to poke with a needle.

As the name of the procedure implies, bone marrow *aspiration* and *biopsy*, it's a two-part procedure.

First, for the part called the aspiration, my procedure is to stick a short needle called an Illinois needle into the iliac crest, and aspirate (suck up) the bone marrow into a syringe. A bone marrow specimen looks like blood, with a little admixed yellow fat. That part of the procedure is pretty much like a phlebotomist drawing blood from a vein in the arm.

For the second part of the procedure, the biopsy, I use a longer, thicker needle called a Jamshidi needle. My procedure is to stick this needle into the iliac crest to collect not only bone marrow, but part of the bone as well.

I was taught that it was preferable to *not* use a Jamshidi needle for the first part of the procedure, the aspiration part, because a Jamshidi needle is about twice as long and wide as the Illinois needle. Therefore, there is too much "dead space" in the needle, which tends to fill up with blood instead of bone marrow, making for a dilute, suboptimal bone-marrow-aspiration specimen.

One more thing: if a patient has too much fat in the hip area, and I cannot reach the iliac crest bone with the Illinois needle or the Jamshidi needle, I can collect the bone marrow aspiration specimen from the sternum, in the chest area, where there is less fat. If I take this approach, however, I cannot use the Jamshidi needle to collect bone marrow because it's too long and thick, which elevates the risks of going through the sternum and puncturing the heart or lungs, with catastrophic results.

So, to summarize, the Illinois needle is used for the aspiration, and the Jamshidi needle is used for the biopsy. Each has an important role to play in the procedure. Also, to collect bone marrow from the sternum, I need an Illinois needle.

For years I happily did these bone marrow specimen collections in the operating room suite of the hospital, using both needles. I was completely satisfied with the Sherwood Bone Marrow Collection kits that the hospital provided for use by medical staff. These kits had everything I needed to do the bone marrow exams: betadine to sterilize the collection site, numbing medicine (xylocaine) with the appropriate needles and syringes, four-by-four gauze sponges...and most importantly, both an Illinois needle and a Jamshidi needle. Everything in these excellent Sherwood kits had a purpose. I was happy, and the patients were happy.

Then, without warning, the hospital changed kits.

It happened this way: I went to the operating room to do a bone marrow procedure. It took a few minutes to get the paperwork done, and to get the patient positioned properly on the operating room table, but then we were ready to get started. The patient was lying face down, breathing through an oxygen mask, the anesthesiologist was poised on the patient's right side, ready to administer propofol through the IV line to put the patient to sleep, and the circulating nurse double-checked that everything was a go. It was time to start. Then my assistant from the lab presented me with a type of bone marrow kit I had never seen before – a different kit from a different vendor. It was obviously cheaper than the Sherwood kits, because it was of lower quality. But I could live with that. What I could not live with though, was that the new kit did not have an Illinois needle, only a Jamshidi needle.

Well, it was too late to cancel the bone marrow procedure, so I plowed on ahead. Since the kit had only a Jamshidi needle, I was forced to use that one needle for both the aspiration and biopsy. First, I aspirated bone marrow through the Jamshidi needle into a syringe and handed the syringe to my assistant; then I proceeded to reposition that same Jamshidi needle for the biopsy. In summary I collected two specimens with one needle instead of two needles. I guess that was one way to reduce costs and help Excel's bottom line.

Unfortunately, that also meant that the quality of the bone marrow specimens went down. Using the big thick Jamshidi needle instead of the missing smaller Illinois needle meant that the bone marrow sucked into the needle was very diluted with blood, making the specimen difficult to interpret. It was easy to miss things and make an incorrect diagnosis. Also, collecting bone marrow from the sternum was no longer an option, because the new kits had no Illinois needles, only Jamshidi needles, which were too big and long to use in the sternum.

This change in bone marrow collection kits was done without any input from me, the person who actually did the procedure, or any other physician who did bone marrow procedures. Instead the decision to make this change to a cheaper, lower-quality product was made by managers and executives in order to lower costs and increase profits. Again, they had no skin in the game. I and physicians like me were the ones on the front lines, trying to collect good-quality bone marrow specimens with suboptimal kits.

Which was frustrating, because collecting good-quality bone marrow specimens couldn't be done. The specimens that I looked at with my microscope were suboptimal, whether collected by me or other physicians. The bone marrow was too diluted by peripheral blood to interpret. It was sad. Patients were being put to sleep by the anesthesia department, with all the risks that entailed, and getting stuck in the butt by a large needle, with all the risks that entailed, for a low-quality bone marrow specimen. And collecting bone marrow from the sternum was no longer an option because no Illinois needle was available in the new kits.

Naively, I asked anyone who would listen: "Is there any way we can go back to the Sherwood kits?"

It turned out that yes, there was a procedure to do that. I could make a request to the Procurement Committee – that they order the Sherwood Bone Marrow Collection kits. So that's what I did. I filled out the forms with my justifications for going back to using the Sherwood kits, or at least making them available as an option.

Of course, the medical justification was easy. The Sherwood kits were a superior product, because they had Illinois needles in them, not just the Jamshidi needles. The Procurement Committee also wanted a letter from me detailing the reasons I preferred the Sherwood product to the new replacement kits. I did that too.

After I provided all this documentation, the Procurement Committee approved my request and forwarded the matter to the Executive Committee, which met a month later. That committee also agreed to make the change back to the Sherwood kits. Finally, a month after that, the board of Excel Pinnacle Hospital rubber-stamped the change back to Sherwood kits. And a few months after the board meeting, Sherwood kits started to arrive to Central Supply, and once again I used these high-quality kits with an Illinois needle to perform bone marrow collection procedures. I was happy.

But not for long. After a few weeks I went to the operating room to do a bone marrow operation, and I was presented with the inferior kit, without an Illinois needle. I asked for a Sherwood kit. None were available.

"What can I do to make them available?" I asked.

The answer was this: "You need to start with a request to the Procurement Committee justifying the change..."

"I already did all that," I said.

"You have to do it again," I was told.

I passed. I mean, what would be the point?

So the end result was that I and everyone else who did bone marrow procedures collected suboptimal specimens, which meant when I or one of the other pathologists examined the bone marrow specimens under the microscope, it was more difficult to make an accurate diagnosis. Or it was impossible to make a diagnosis at all, and the specimen was signed out as "nondiagnostic," which didn't make anyone happy – me, the patient, or the clinicians taking care of the patient.

Why didn't Excel Pinnacle Hospital do as I asked, and help me take care of patients by providing high-quality bone marrow kits instead of providing inadequate kits to me and the rest of the physicians? The same answer I have already mentioned: Because nothing was more important to Bart Magnum and the executives of Excel Corp than meeting their numbers, and there were two ways of meeting their numbers – increase revenue (e.g., more paying patients in the hospital) or decrease costs (e.g., cheaper bone marrow kits). Of course, the money saved by buying the cheaper bone marrow kits amounted to very little, but that mentality extended to other equipment and supplies – lumbar puncture kits, sutures, operating room supplies, lab equipment, X-ray equipment, and everything else needed to run a hospital – meant that costs went down and profits went up.

This made Bart Magnum and the other executives at Excel Corp very happy. We're talking big bucks here. Bart made a seven-figure income. The rest of the executives at Excel Pinnacle made an income well into the high six figures. And the executives at Excel Corp headquarters in downtown Midwest City had similar high incomes. And the best part was that they had no responsibility or liability to worry about. I never heard of an Excel executive getting sued for malpractice or anything else. Only the physicians had such worries.

The Mission Statement of Excel Corp was "Above all else we are committed to patient well-being, and high quality healthcare." I read it every day I went to work. It was posted at the entrance of the hospital and on several of the corridor walls.

CHAPTER 9

But, but, but, why didn't we, the doctors, fight back against all these deleterious changes that happened at Excel Pinnacle Hospital? Or the doctors at virtually every other hospital in the country, where the same things were happening – why didn't they resist and fight for better patient care? Why didn't the physicians *do* something?

Good questions, but I don't have good answers, because physicians shouldn't be that easy to push around. After all, for the most part physicians are smart, educated people. Only physicians have the education, training, experience, and know-how to make diagnoses and treat patients. Everything that happens at a hospital revolves around the doctors. Without the work of physicians, the healthcare system would grind to a halt. Nothing would happen without the docs. That means physicians should have a lot of power. But they don't. Or at least they don't use it.

Instead, they are ignored and beat down by healthcare executives with MBAs or other business degrees, and attorneys and other managers and bureaucrats. These individuals working at hospitals, insurance companies, and regulatory agencies must laugh their heads off at physicians for putting up with all the crap they dish out. They must marvel at how easy it is to push us around.

Doctors don't go on strike, stage slowdowns, show up for protests, or demonstrate for better working conditions and pay. They do nothing of the sort. They just show up for work every day, doing the best they can, under increasingly intolerable working conditions, for an income that stays flat or goes down each year. Why in the world don't physicians use the powers at their disposal? Well, I'm a physician, and I have worked with physicians for fifty years, and although some of what follows is conjecture, here are my ideas about why doctors have been so timid:

1. The changes for the worse were gradual, over a long period of time. In the 1950s and 1960s doctors had a lot of power, probably too much power. It's interesting to view movies made back in those times, and watch doctors do incredibly arrogant things, like prescribe very potent medicines such as powerful tranquilizers and not even tell the patient what the drug is or what it's for, especially if the patient is female. The philosophy was that the doctor knew best. Actually, it was a form of control. But over time that kind of power and control eroded. There was not a definite time when physicians went from very powerful to not so powerful. The changes were incremental. Describing the reduction of physicians' authority and control by the government, insurance companies, hospital companies, and others would take a book of its own. The changes were cloaked in euphemisms like "efficiencies," "best practices," and "cost savings." And how could doctors say anything was wrong with that!? And some doctors not only acquiesced to the changes but led the way by writing the new guidelines and policies. The end result was a series of algorithms that doctors had to follow, which left doctors simply following guidelines other "experts" had written, rather than doing what each doctor thought was best for his or her patient, i.e., actually practicing medicine. Also, the Golden Rule applied: those with the gold made the rules. The insurance companies, government payers, and hospitals had the gold (the money) and made the rules. Oh, it was wonderful at first when Medicare and Medicaid and the various insurance companies came along and reliably paid the doctors for services rendered, instead of patients who might or might not be able to pay – no longer were there bad debts, unpaid bills, and free care. But since these entities were paying the bills, eventually they made the rules.

2. Physicians hate conflict. A typical physician will do just about anything to avoid conflict – take all kinds of verbal abuse, do eight hours of extra work to appease a slacker, and get along

by going along. The persons who get accepted into medical school and graduate, make it through residency, and eventually become practicing physicians tend to be conscientious, hardworking, obedient, and scholarly learners who do as they are taught and try to please others and follow the rules. There are probably many reasons that such is the case. My sense is that many physicians come from dysfunctional families where they played the role of hero with an intense desire to succeed in life and smooth over troubles and pretend that everything is normal. Such individuals are able to survive the competition to get into medical school and become physicians. Those who try to become physicians but like conflict or rebel against authority, well, they do not become physicians; they are weeded out. They don't graduate from medical school or finish their residencies or get medical licenses. It's quite simple, really: people who like to fight don't end up as physicians; they become lawyers, insurance company executives, or hospital administrators.

3. Doctors are not smart enough to figure out what to do. It pains me to write this, because I used to be proud to be a physician, and I used to think doctors were smart. When I started medical school fifty years ago, my sense of my fellow students was that they were very intelligent. I had to work hard to keep up. I had similar impressions during my residency and when I started out in private practice. Physicians seemed to me to not only be well educated, but reasonably clever as well. I don't think that anymore. In many ways, I think doctors are very naive and simple. Physicians are able to understand, assimilate, and apply some scientific and medical concepts, which is a skill, a "knack" if you will, that enables them to learn how to perform rather complex medical maneuvers – operations, procedures, diagnoses, treatments and the like. But that's pretty much the extent of their learning and judgment. I have not appreciated other manifestations of above-

average intelligence in physicians. I have encountered virtually none with exceptional verbal abilities. Most physicians I know are horrible writers. Nor have I run into many physicians with mathematical abilities that impress me. Physicians I know tend to not be particularly well-read or literate. Their knowledge of philosophy is minimal. As a group, physicians are so ignorant of the arts that it makes me weep. And physicians with political smarts are very rare and exotic creatures. The end result is that doctors are easily taken advantage of by healthcare executives who work for hospitals or insurance companies, who are greedy and ruthless and have better political and management skills. It's not a fair contest. It's a mismatch.

CHAPTER 10

I liked the time I spent in the walkway connecting Excel Pinnacle Hospital to the medical office building across the street. Sometimes when I made my way through the walkway, I would stop, lean forward on the handrails, and just look into the distance. I liked to rest my eyes after looking through a microscope so long and often.

The topography around Pathfinder was the topography of the Great Plains of the American Midwest – flat. This meant I had a clear look at the horizon and, if I had time to look, saw magnificent sunrises and sunsets. If I looked to the east, I could almost see the skyline of Midwest City thirty miles distant, and looking to the west, I could see the Rocky Mountains hundreds of miles in the distance. Well, almost. The hospital was on the edge of town, and I could see the adjacent countryside – a pool table topped with green pastures separated by fields of corn, houses, and silos.

And tornados, I could see them coming in the distance, so I had time to get to a safe place. The one we had in 2015 was typical. The tornado came on a day in May, which started out sunny, still, and glorious – a nice change from the usual brutal winter and cold rainy spring. The sky was a blue dome, without a cloud, interrupted only by the sun to the east. Then clouds formed in the west, white at first, then turning darker. Breezes blew into town, rustling the leaves of the elm trees. As the breezes turned stronger, rows of white birch trees swayed back and forth in response to the gusting haphazard winds. The clouds were not dramatic at first, but then became threatening. They turned from white to gray, then with splotches of black. All at once the sky turned yellow and green all at the same time. Out of this yellow and green collage, a black/gray funnel formed and headed toward Pathfinder. I could see it coming. So could everyone else. When it hit Pathfinder, it was awful, with a lot of damage, but no one was hurt. Everyone found shelter because we could see it coming. We were warned and prepared.

In retrospect, I should have seen part two of this story coming, the tornado. The signs were all there. After all, I saw what happened to the ER docs and the hospitalists. What happened to them was likely to happen to me. The ER docs and hospitalists warned me to get out while I could, with my reputation and assets intact. What happened to me with the bone marrow kits was also a harbinger of things to come.

So I should not have been surprised at the tornado that disrupted my life in 2017. Too bad. If I had foreseen what was in store for me that year, I would have retired in 2016, when I was sixty-seven years old. I had paid my dues, done my time. I should have sold Pathology Services and walked away, kept my head down, stayed out of trouble, and enjoyed my retirement.

But I didn't do that. I kept working well into my late sixties, an age when most physicians are retired. I continued to examine specimens, run my pathology laboratory, and look through my microscope. I liked the work, and I liked helping people. Why quit?

Then a tornado hit, and I was unprepared.

PART TWO

2017–Present

CHAPTER 1

My fellow doctors were hurting. They no longer felt like professionals, but like cogs in a machine. They went to medical school to learn how to take care of patients, and during their internships and residencies, their teachers set high standards for them, so the doctors set high standards for themselves. They wanted to do a good job. But under the working conditions set by the hospitals and the insurance companies, they couldn't do that anymore.

Some physicians knew that I had written three books. "Tell the story," they said. "Write down what is happening to us."

"No one will read it," I replied. "No one cares what happens to a bunch of rich doctors. Physicians don't have it so rough. Warehouse workers at Amazon, cashiers at Walmart, and drivers for UPS – now they have it rough. Or individuals working on the line at a meatpacking plant or an automobile factory. Readers might have sympathy for those people, the real essential workers of our society, but not doctors who have it pretty good and wouldn't last a day at a real job."

So when the ER docs lost their jobs, I didn't tell that story. The change didn't really affect me that much. And when the hospitalists were fired, I didn't make a fuss because that change really didn't affect me either.

But when the same forces came after me, it was time to tell the tale.

CHAPTER 2

The story I am about to tell is simple, although the details are technical and arcane. There are three characters:

1. A giant hospital company called Excel Corp.

2. Me, one man, an owner of a small company, Pathology Services.

3. A giant insurance company called Merciful.

The three of us conducted business in harmony for forty years, living in symbiosis, like a coral reef.

Excel Hospital Corp owned over three hundred hospitals in the country. Each of these hospitals needed pathology laboratories and pathologists to examine the tissue specimens removed by surgeons. This examination was done to determine what diseases were present – cancer, infection, or some other diagnosis. Because most community/suburban hospitals weren't large enough to have their own pathology laboratory, they sent their specimens to an independent pathology lab. That independent pathology lab had the staff to process the tissue, and doctors (pathologists) to make the diagnoses, which were reported to the hospital and the patient's doctors so the doctors would know how to treat the patient. My lab, Pathology Services, was one such lab, and I was one such pathologist. Three other pathologists were also employed by my company. Pathology Services had a contract to examine tissue specimens for Excel Pinnacle Hospital, one of Excel Corp's hospitals.

Merciful was the largest health insurance company in the state, by far. The insurance company paid my lab, Pathology Services, a pathology lab fee to cover the costs of processing each tissue specimen. The insurance company also paid the pathologist a fee for examining each specimen and reporting the interpretations and diagnoses. Simply put, Pathology Services sent two bills to Merciful – one for the costs of running the lab, and another for the work of the pathologist (me or one of the other pathologists employed by Pathology Services) who examined the specimen and made the interpretations and diagnoses.

For over forty years, since the time that Excel Pinnacle Hospital was built, the three of us – Pathology Services, Excel Hospital Corp, and Merciful Insurance – worked together, and everyone was happy.

At Pathology Services we were happy, because we made a reasonable profit after paying the salaries of our employees and operating costs.

Excel Pinnacle Hospital was happy because Pathology Services provided Excel Pinnacle Hospital patients with high-quality specimen interpretations and diagnoses, which were indispensable for good patient care. And the best part for Excel Pinnacle was that the bills for all this were paid for by Merciful Insurance. Excel Pinnacle didn't pay a thing.

Finally, Merciful Insurance Company was happy because even after paying the bills from Pathology Services and other providers of healthcare, there was plenty of money left over to pay very high salaries to its employees, with billions of dollars left over for "reserves," i.e., profits.

In summary, it was a good deal for everyone.

Then Merciful got greedy. Merciful decided that it could save money by simply not paying my pathology lab the costs of running the laboratory. Oh, they were willing to pay one of the bills, the fee to the pathologist/doctor for examining the tissue. But they stopped paying the other bill, the fee to cover the costs of running the laboratory. Merciful contended that the costs of running my pathology lab were paid to Excel Pinnacle Hospital, in a "bundled payment." Merciful evidently "forgot" to let Excel Pinnacle know that, or Excel Pinnacle was informed, but decided to keep the money, because Excel Pinnacle never paid me a dime for any pathology costs whatsoever. Both Merciful and Excel wanted me to "eat the costs" of running the laboratory and provide those services for free.

Stripped of the healthcare jargon, the fraud was that simple – by refusing to pay my valid charges, the Merciful Insurance Company and Excel Corp wanted my pathology lab to provide something to them for nothing. That was bad enough, to not get paid for work my pathology lab did. But there were worse consequences. Providing such services for free was against healthcare law; accepting such conditions would have been a bribe from Pathology Services to Merciful and Excel, or a kickback, or whatever name you want to give this crime. What Merciful and Excel did was illegal. They broke the law. And they got away with it.

CHAPTER 3

April 2017

My war with the Merciful Insurance Company started with a sneak attack. It happened while I was working at the hospital, examining tissue from a patient's left breast, trying to make a diagnosis for the surgeon.

The specimen looked innocent enough on the outside – bright yellow fat the color of the sun interspersed with strands of white breast tissue, like thin clouds. But beneath this nonthreatening soft surface, my gloved hands palpated a hard mass that felt like a rock. It felt like cancer.

Not all was lost, however. Other disease processes, say a benign cyst, can mimic cancer. A cyst is a fluid-filled sac that commonly occurs in the breast. The fluid can accumulate and increase the pressure the way air fills a balloon, getting bigger and bigger, stretching the cyst walls until there's a hard mass that masquerades as cancer.

Unfortunately, when I cut into the mass with my scalpel, I did not see any fluid, and there was no cyst. Instead, my scalpel blade encountered a solid grayish white tumor/mass. It was about two inches in diameter, although it was difficult to get an accurate measurement because it was poorly circumscribed with gray tentacles that extended from the mass into the adjacent normal breast tissue, like a "crab," which is a centuries-old nickname for cancer. The lesion looked like cancer, wild and unrestrained, which it was, evil incarnate.

I sampled the tumor tissue and placed a small thin piece on a chuck (a one-inch-diameter gold-colored metal block). I put the chuck with the tissue in a machine called a cryostat, a freezer that housed a very sharp knife blade. At minus 20 degrees, it didn't take long for the tissue to freeze and stick to the chuck. I placed the chuck with attached tissue on a holder that could be advanced by a part of the cryostat called a microtome, with the result that the blade could cut a very thin piece of tissue, which I placed on a glass microscope slide. I took that slide over to a set of chemicals and dyes and dipped the slide through each chemical, one after another. Then I covered the stained tissue with a thin glass coverslip. I felt like Mr. Wizard performing black magic.

I took the slide to my office and looked at it under the microscope. My phone was ringing; I could see with my caller ID that the caller was Sela Ray, my business manager. I ignored the ringing phone. Nothing was more important at that moment than looking at this slide with my microscope, concentrating, and making a diagnosis.

The diagnosis was cancer. The phone kept ringing. I paid no attention to it. Instead, I documented my diagnosis of breast cancer. Then I hurried upstairs to the operating room suite. I put on a surgical mask and cap and walked into the operating room. Dr. Anderson Spickard was closing the breast wound with sutures; he made dramatic loops with the suture needle and tied the knots with a flourish. The man knew how to be a surgeon.

I looked at Anderson and said, "It's what you thought it would be: invasive mammary carcinoma." I showed him my report and then placed it in the patient's chart.

Dr. Spickard wasn't surprised. He turned to the circulating OR nurse and said, "Get the chapel ready for a family conference."

When I got back to my office, the phone was still ringing, and the caller ID still said Sela Ray. I picked up the phone. "What's going on?" I said.

Sela said, "I feel sick, like I'm going to throw up." Her tone of voice matched her words – it was shaking, quavering, like she was in shock.

"What happened?"

"I just received a bunch of letters from Merciful Insurance, hundreds of them, thousands of them, demanding money!"

"How much money are we talking about?"

"Hard to tell. I haven't added up the amounts, but at least several hundred thousand dollars."

I said, "I have to hang up. I can't talk."

"We have to fight this."

"I know."

This first attack by Merciful was a blizzard of small envelopes, which buried me. Each envelope contained a short simple letter on a small single sheet of cheap computer paper, about the size of an index card. We received thousands of these communications, each with the same format. Here is an example:

AUDIT
Patient: Rob Sorley
Specimen: Appendix
Service billed: Pathology Lab Service for tissue processing
Merciful Payment $25.00
Amount which should have been paid: $0
Amount to be refunded to Merciful Insurance Company: $25.00

Provider Audit

That was it; there was no other information in these communications. I've left nothing out. The only signature was "Provider Audit" – no name of a person, department, nothing. It was bizarre – a faceless, nameless entity named "Provider Audit" was seeking so much money from me that it would destroy my business. I never heard or saw anything like it in my life. It seemed like fiction, something out of a Franz Kafka novel, specifically his book *The Trial*, which starts with these words: "Someone must have slandered Josef K, for one morning, without having done anything wrong, he was arrested."

My nightmare started in a similar fashion – to paraphrase Kafka: One morning, having done nothing wrong, "Provider Audit" and other entities conspired to destroy my business...and me.

In Kafka's book, Josef K never receives an explanation for his arrest or anything else that happens to him. The book ends when two men kill Josef K "like a dog" with hands to the throat and a knife to the heart. I hoped to avoid a similar fate.

But it seemed like these letters from "Provider Audit" would never stop. During the next several days, I received thousands of such letters.

I had received no warning that these letters were coming – no notice of a change in contract terms, no notice of a change in policies, no phone calls, no alerts...nothing. I had not been given a chance to communicate with Merciful or negotiate with the company or reason with its executives. Instead, these letters were a surprise attack that threatened my company, like the sneak attack on Pearl Harbor that brought America into World War II.

The second attack followed a few days later. I received six follow-up summary letters, each on high-quality stationery with the Merciful Insurance Company letterhead. Each letter had the same format – only the dates and dollar amounts differed. Here is one of the six letters I received:

> Summary of Merciful Overpayment Notification of 4/2/2017
> Pathology Services
> P.O. Box 0000
> Pathfinder, Midwest State, 76820
>
> Dear Pathology Services, P.C.:
> Merciful Insurance determined that an overpayment was made to you in the amount of $10,931.03.
> No action by you is required at this time. Pursuant to Midwest State Code Annotated Section 56-7-110 Merciful will attempt to recover the overpayment through and offset to your charges, beginning 45 days from the date of this letter.
> If you prefer an immediate payment of this overpayment to you please write RECOUP IN LARGE LETTERS on the subject line of the remittance check, and include a copy of this letter.
> If you think overpayment did not occur, you must ask for a reconsideration of this audit decision. Reconsideration must be requested in writing within 30 days from the date of this

letter by sending a copy of this letter, the pertinent medical records for the dates of service on the claim(s), and supporting information along with your request to:

Merciful Insurance Compan2 Mountain Pass Way Suite 0019 Midwest City, Midwest State, 76821

Additional information regarding recovery of claims or overpayments is available in the Merciful Provider Administration Manual and Commercial and Medicare and Medicaid Bundling Rules located on the company's website. In addition there are other rights available that are set forth in Midwest State Code Annotated Section 56-7-111.

If you have any questions about your claim adjustment status, please call the Provider Service Line at 1-800-000-0000.

Sincerely,
Provider Audit Department.

Notes: This pathology lab service was provided in a hospital. This pathology lab service would have been reimbursed to the hospital.

I received a total of six letters each with the same wording, differing only with respect to the dates and dollar amounts. The dates and dollar amounts in each of these letters was as follows:

1. April 2 ($10,931.03)
2. April 6 ($252,358.66)
3. April 10 ($95,437.71)
4. April 12 ($12,583.78)
5. April 19 ($313,131.19)
6. April 20 ($83,212.91)

These summary letters were accompanied by yet more documents – hundreds, no, *thousands* of printed spreadsheets itemizing patient data and charges and the amount of money we owed Merciful. To summarize, everything that Merciful had paid Pathology Services for pathology lab services – *work that we had done* – had to be paid back, every last cent. This was not doable.

How to convey what a shock this was? It was as if you sold your house to someone and used the proceeds to build a new house. Then when the new house was finished and you moved in, the entity that purchased your old house wanted their money back *and* kept possession of the house you sold.

I added up the amounts of money these communications said we owed to Merciful. The total was $767,655.28. This amount was more than the annual profits of Pathology Services, much more. I made a good living as a pathologist and an owner of Pathology Services, but nowhere close to the income needed to pay such a debt. It would destroy my business.

Worse, it would destroy me. See, you may be thinking that all I had to do was close the doors of Pathology Services and retire. No big deal, right? Small businesses go bankrupt every day.

But I couldn't do that. Pathology Services stored microscopic slides and paraffin blocks from patients. Every day we received requests from doctors and patients to do further studies on these specimens – e.g., send the slides to an expert for a second opinion, do additional tests or special stains on the tissues, compare the tumor from a previous specimen (e.g., the lung) to a metastatic tumor in a present specimen (e.g., liver tissue). The slides, paraffin blocks, and tissues stored in my pathology lab, whether for one day or ten years, were used for ongoing diagnoses and treatments. Closing my pathology lab would make these patient specimens unavailable. This was not an option. Patients and their doctors would be incredibly angry if these specimens were not available for additional studies needed for patient care. Closing Pathology Services, locking the doors, and walking away would make me vulnerable to malpractice lawsuits (or worse) from countless irate patients and their families who couldn't get access to the tissues from previous surgical operations for these additional studies. And for these sick patients, this was often a life-or-death issue.

Why was Merciful doing this to me, trying to put me out of business and destroy me? There was no explanation – no phone call, no discussion, no notice, no new contract. Nothing.

The only clue was in the "Notes" section at the bottom of each of the summary letters, which said: "The pathology lab service was provided in a hospital and would have been reimbursed to the hospital." That's it. Nothing else.

The first sentence was a lie. The pathology lab service was **not** provided in a hospital, but was provided in my Pathology Services laboratory, which was located several miles from the hospital.

The second sentence, "The pathology lab bill would have been reimbursed to the hospital," was ambiguous – was Excel Pinnacle hospital paid the money or not? If the money was not paid to the hospital, then Merciful was totally out of line coming after me for the money. Alternatively, if this statement meant that Merciful mistakenly paid Excel Pinnacle Hospital for work done by my pathology lab, then obviously Merciful should get Excel Pinnacle Hospital to pay back the money, not me.

So why didn't Merciful do that, go after the hospital instead of my pathology lab? And of course, the answer is obvious – my pathology lab was a weaker opponent. Excel was a big company, even bigger than Merciful, and if Merciful went after Excel for the money, Excel would fight back, with comparable resources. Excel had a legal department full of attorneys and paralegals who had nothing better to do than fight with Merciful. In addition, in Pathfinder and in Midwest City, almost every law firm of any size did business with Excel. It would be difficult to impossible for Merciful to find an attorney to hire; most firms would decline the case because of conflicts with the legal work they got from Excel. A battle between Merciful and Excel would have been a fair fight, with the edge to Excel.

But Merciful had no such worries about me. My pathology lab was a small business, with one general practice attorney on retainer, who advised me on contracts, personnel decisions and the like. That's it.

It was David versus Goliath.

Finally, the third attack was a "justification letter." The letter simply stated that since Medicare didn't pay my pathology lab the pathology lab costs, then neither should Merciful. The letter was written on paper with the Merciful Insurance letterhead and went like this:

Justification of Report of Audit Findings
Pathology Services
P.O. Box 0000
Pathfinder, Midwest State 76820

Audit number 33438
Audit Period: last two years
Type of Audit: Desk Audit

AUDIT RESULTS

Summary

Per Medicare Claims Processing Manual Chapter 16: Laboratory Services effective on or after July 12, 2012, only the hospital may bill for the pathology lab costs provided to an inpatient or outpatient.
A listing of the claims audited and identified for adjustment follows. Claims identified for adjustments have been forwarded to our financial recovery units for handling.
In the event you wish to dispute our findings, please submit a written request for reconsideration citing the audit number above, and why you disagree. Please include any supporting documentation to:

Merciful Insurance
2 Mountain Pass Way Suite 0019
Midwest City, Midwest State, 76821

In the event the original findings are overturned or modified as a result of the dispute process, Merciful will refund recouped payments accordingly.
Thank you for your cooperation during our auditing process.

That was it. I've reproduced the letter the way I received it. Notice the letter was unsigned – no signature, no name, no department… nothing. Not even "Provider Audit."

I continued to feel like a character in a Kafka novel or George Orwell's book *1984*. I hardly know where to begin to detail the abuses and falsehoods.

First, the word "audit" in this context had as much validity as the misnomer "Ministry of Truth" did in Orwell's book. What Merciful did was more like a confiscation or robbery or…coercion – yes, that's the word I'm looking for. Merciful did not do an "audit," i.e., an independent examination by impartial inspectors. No, this was a group of bureaucrats and executives from Merciful that decided they wanted to take money from me.

No, it was worse than that. Merciful didn't want to just take money from me. They wanted to bully my pathology lab into insolvency and destroy my company, which I spent almost forty years building. If I survived at all, I would be an indentured servant.

And "per Medicare" was irrelevant. What Medicare did or did not do was not applicable to Merciful. Medicare was a government program. Merciful was a private company.

It was true that Medicare did not pay my pathology lab costs. Medicare paid that money to Excel Pinnacle Hospital, which passed those reimbursements to Pathology Services, because we did the work.

But Medicare was the only payer that required the hospitals to bill for the pathology lab costs and either keep the money or pass it on to the lab that actually incurred the lab costs. Importantly, this situation was unique to Medicare, which was a government payer, not a private insurance company. Medicare had used its political influence to advocate for a series of laws passed by Congress that required hospitals to bear the pathology lab costs. Of course, doing this cut down on expenses for Medicare, which were passed on to the hospitals. Good deal for Medicare, if not such a good deal for the hospitals.

However, it was an Orwellian leap to say that since Medicare didn't pay the pathology lab costs to me, neither should Merciful. Merciful was NOT Medicare, which again, is a government program. Merciful was a private insurance company, like Blue Cross, United,

Cigna, Aetna and every other private insurance company, which paid all fees and costs directly to me, not the hospital. All the other private insurance companies paid my pathology lab costs directly to me. And until these shenanigans, so did Merciful. Now Merciful was trying to use non-applicable Medicare policies to cheat my pathology lab out of the money they owed me for services my pathology lab provided Merciful-insured patients. It was brazen and illegal.

It was as if American Airlines or United Airlines or some other company demanded *retroactively* the same terms from Boeing that the Defense Department got, ignoring that the Defense Department is a government entity, and the airlines are private companies.

It's as if an independent plumber had a contract to take care of an apartment complex, which was done for several years, and that plumber billed the customer an hourly rate for doing the work and also billed the apartment owner for any equipment and parts needed – new water heater, replacing faucets, valves, pumps...Then, years later, *after* years of service, the owner of the apartment complex decided he was only going to pay the hourly rate to the plumber for doing the work (i.e., pathologist professional fee) but won't pay for the parts used to do the job – the faucet, the valve, the washer (i.e., the costs of running the lab). Continuing the analogy, it would be like the apartment owner then taking back the previously paid money and demanding that the plumber continue to work under those money-losing conditions.

If you, dear reader, are confused, you are not losing your mind. That's what Merciful was counting on: complexity to hide their unlawful behavior. What Merciful was doing was exploiting ambiguities in payments and contracts to contend that Merciful didn't have to pay me the costs that my pathology lab incurred while providing services to Merciful-insured patients. Of course, the management at Merciful knew what they were doing was wrong. What Merciful was doing to me was unethical. In fact, it was illegal.

The corruption was off the charts. The approximately $750,000.00 hit would bankrupt me. And what amazed me was that this amount of money was pocket change to Merciful, not even a rounding error on the company's income and expense statements. Merciful's revenues were

8.93 billion dollars a year. They had 4 billion dollars of cash in the bank. They had six thousand employees.

Pathology Services had revenues of five million dollars a year. We had no cash reserves – at the end of each fiscal year, we emptied out the coffers with bonuses for the employees, including me. We had twenty employees.

What got me at the time, and still gets me, is this: Merciful obviously had the resources to help me provide good medical care to its patients, which I had done for about four decades, sacrificing time with family and friends, neglecting my health, and giving my all to my profession. But Merciful did not treat me like a professional, like a partner. They treated me with contempt. This was the boot of the strong on the neck of the weak.

I had to fight.

CHAPTER 4

April 2017

But how to fight? That was part of the mismatch. Unfortunately, during medical school, there were no classes about how to go about defending your medical practice from the attack of a corrupt corporation. Courses with titles of *How to Find and Hire an Attorney* or *Strategies to Fight Corruption* were not offered. Same thing with my residency training – I learned a lot about medicine and science and how to take care of patients, but nothing about how to run a business, or how to defend yourself against an unscrupulous insurance company.

My foe was formidable, with considerable legal resources at its disposal. To begin with Merciful had an in-house legal department full of attorneys and paralegals available to advise the company on routine legal matters. I suspect this was the genesis of my problems. Undoubtedly, when they had some time on their hands, the Merciful lawyers met with the executives in the "Managed Care Operations Department" to brainstorm ideas to increase profits and came up with this harebrained scheme to "audit" my lab and raise money that way.

In addition to this in-house legal expertise, Merciful had on retainer a large multinational law firm based in Midwest City, which employed hundreds of attorneys ready to go to war for Merciful if needed.

In contrast, my pathology lab had no in-house legal department. I had one attorney on retainer, Ray Scott, who was in a six-member firm, although Ray was the only attorney I dealt with. Pathology Services paid him a monthly retainer, and for that fee he was available to us for legal consultations at an hourly rate. Ray was a "Jack of all trades" lawyer who could do things like review and modify contracts, advise on personnel issues, and do general practice legal work. However, with respect to this fight with Merciful, he was no help.

"I don't do that kind of work," he said.

"Do you know anyone who does?" I asked.

"No."

I was on my own.

I did know of one law firm, located in Maine, that might be able to help me. Marion Daniel, LLP, was a firm specializing in healthcare law, including taking on Merciful. Ten years earlier the pathologists in Midwest State took group action against Merciful in a quarrel having to do with reimbursement. Marion Daniel, LLP provided the legal assistance. As one of the smallest pathology groups in the state, I played a minimal role in this statewide quarrel, which was eventually settled by arbitration. Nevertheless, I did meet the managing partner of the firm, the appropriately named Marion Daniel. My impression, and that of other pathologists in the state, was that the firm had good lawyers, but that they were expensive.

Expensive or not, I needed them. I phoned Marion Daniel. He remembered me and said his firm was willing to help. My case was assigned to an associate attorney in his firm.

Quickly though, I realized that using a law firm in Maine was not going to work for several reasons. First, I couldn't hear very well what the associate attorney was saying due to a poor long-distance phone connection. Second, her New England accent was much different from the generic Midwestern English I was used to, and I had difficulty understanding her. Third, during our first few conversations, she used headphones, which were comfortable for her, but resulted in a lag in her responses to my comments, which drove me nuts. Last, but not least, the logistical challenges of working with a firm in faraway Maine were going to be insurmountable, in my opinion. For example, right off the bat the associate attorney wanted me to send to her a copy of our contract with Merciful, all correspondence with Merciful, samples of the requests for payment, and all the other documents pertinent to the case. These were reasonable requests. But that meant Sela and I would have to run down all this paperwork, make copies, and then ship all this stuff to Maine. Too much. It was going to be hard enough to fight Merciful without these logistical challenges. The Marion Daniel law firm was not an option. I needed local help.

So I phoned Reynolds Price, who had been my partner, a co-owner of Pathology Services, until he retired about ten years earlier. He was a little older than me and very wise. I phoned him and asked him if he had any ideas.

He did. Reynolds reminded me of Walter Sneed, an attorney in nearby Midwest City, who had helped us out with a Medicaid matter back in the late 1990s. I never met Walter Sneed because Reynolds worked on the case without my help. Nevertheless, I remembered that Walter had done a good job for us. Reynolds suggested that I give Walter Sneed a call.

I did. I gave Mr. Sneed a brief explanation of my problem, and he was willing to help me if there were no conflicts with the interests of any of his firm's other clients. An absence of conflicts was no sure thing. Walter Sneed's firm, Cordell and Cochran, was a large one with many attorneys and many clients. Also, Merciful and Excel tended to hog the attorneys in the region, because their legal needs were insatiable. They were always fighting somebody. Sometimes they were fighting each other. Nevertheless, a day later Mr. Sneed let me know there were no conflicts. I had myself an attorney.

The first order of business was to pay the man. That started with a $5,000.00 retainer fee. This money would be used up at the rate of $350.00 an hour, with any unused money to be returned to me. Yeah, right. The $5,000.00 was gone.

The second thing to do was complete some paperwork, including a document titled "CONFIRMATION OF REPRESENTATION." On it there was a place for me to sign, as well as places for my three employee pathologists to sign. Getting that done was a little problematic for three reasons:

1. I was afraid word would get out about my conflict with Merciful, and I liked to keep a low profile – just keep my head down and do my job.
2. Pathologists are wary about signing stuff, so I was worried some of my colleagues would be reluctant to sign the document.

3. In addition, I was not on particularly good terms with one of my pathologist employees whose mission at Pathology Services seemed to me to be to do the least amount of work for the most amount of pay (I am aware that everyone has that attitude to some extent, including me). Nevertheless, my perception was that she didn't do anything unless there was a clear and present benefit for her.

As it turned out, there were no problems. As far as potential problem number one, if word got out, no one seemed to care. With respect to concern number two, everyone signed without incident. With respect to concern number three, my challenging employee merely listened to my explanation without comment and then said, "Where do I sign?"

The next thing I had to do was fire the Maine attorneys. I phoned Marion Daniel and told him what I was doing – that I was going with a local firm. I asked him to send me a bill for any work his firm had already done (which he certainly did – the bill was $1,100.00). I followed up the phone call with an e-mail to him so that the termination was documented.

This is the life of a healer?

CHAPTER 5

April 2017

Walter started on the case immediately. Sela and I sent him the pertinent documents of the case, which he quickly reviewed. On April 22, a Saturday, Walter sent me this e-mail:

"Jack and Sela, it looks like the Medicare provision cited to support the audit reports does not even apply to you. Let me know if I am missing something."

I replied immediately:

"Walter, of course I agree that this provision does not apply to us. That situation is NOT RELEVANT to our situation, because Excel Pinnacle Hospital does not bear those lab costs. We do. Also, Excel Pinnacle Hospital passes on to us the Medicare payments to us for our lab costs. Excel Pinnacle DOES NOT pass on to us any Merciful payments for our lab costs."

CHAPTER 6

April 2017

It was time to meet Walter Sneed face-to-face, so Sela and I made an appointment to drive over to his office in Midwest City.

Sela, my business manager, was in her late thirties, and her background was on-the-job training. Her formal education ended with a high school diploma, but she had a PhD in getting things done. When Sela was eighteen years old, she started working for Pathology Services as a courier. Then she became a clerk in the business office. She was eventually promoted to office manager, and then when our business manager moved away, Sela took over the position. Sela kept getting more responsible positions because she was energetic and smart. Most of all, she was one of those people who just knew what to do. That kind of person is rare in my experience. Sela was invaluable in this battle against Merciful.

On the day of the appointment we drove from Pathfinder to Walter's office located in the heart of downtown Midwest City on the nineteenth floor of the Republic Bank Building, which was across the street from the Renaissance Hotel. Walter had instructed us to park in the parking garage attached to the bank and then take an elevator to his office. This was harder to do than it sounds. Sela and I brought the pertinent documents with us: the demand letters, the "audit" documents, financial statements, contracts, and all the communications with Merciful – a lot of paper, so much that Sela and I had to use two dollies to transport all of it to Walter's office. Luckily we were in reasonably good shape. I went swimming every day. Sela went skiing year round with her husband and three sons – water skiing in the summer and snow skiing in the winter.

Walter's receptionist took us to a conference room, which was furnished in a minimalist fashion — a large oval wood table with matching wood chairs. That was it — no windows. The white walls were bare — no paintings, pictures, or anything else to break the bleak monotony. This room was designed for work.

Which Sela and I proceeded to do. We unloaded the papers from the dollies and put them on the table. When we were finished, the documents covered the whole table. Since the table pretty much occupied the entire room, it was fair to say that we were in a room full of paperwork.

Walter was punctual. He was a tall lean bookish-appearing man with gray hair expertly parted on the left, nary a hair out of place. He had the appearance of a modern-day Ichabod Crane dressed as a lawyer — dark suit, white shirt, and a checkered black and gold tie, the colors of Ivory University, his alma mater located in Midwest City. Ivory University was nicknamed the "Harvard of the Midwest."

Walter was not overwhelmed by the number of documents — the more, the better. He handled each document delicately and carefully, like a jeweler handles his inventory of necklaces, rings, and bracelets. Walter examined them very carefully and very slowly. He was studious and meticulous. Jumping ahead in the story, I can tell you that over the coming weeks and months, this careful plodding approach to the case would drive me nuts.

Fortunately, however, this first meeting did not last long, certainly not more than an hour. We had already discussed on the phone much of what was in the paperwork. This trip to Walter's office was mainly to get the needed documents to Walter. The brief meeting also served as a get-acquainted face-to-face meeting so that Sela and I could match Walter's voice with his face, and Walter could to the same with us during future phone calls and other communications. During this conflict with Merciful, I would have more contact with Walter than I did with anyone else, even members of my family. I barely had time for anything else.

CHAPTER 7

April 2017

Walter had a lawyer acquaintance, David Taft, who worked in Merciful's legal department. In the past Walter had worked with Mr. Taft on matters similar to mine. To hear Walter tell it, the two of them often worked together efficiently and quickly to resolve disagreements to the satisfaction of all parties involved, without litigation or other measures. My fondest hope was that Walter could do that for me. I hoped that he could make a few phone calls and make this huge problem go away.

Walter sent this e-mail to Donald Taft, with a copy to me:

"Donald, I'm working with Pathology Services, PC, and its physicians related to the attached overpayment demand. Would you have time to discuss this briefly next week?

My initial review indicates that the claim is off base. I would be glad to discuss why I think so, and hear your thoughts.

The Reconsideration Appeal is due in early May. Let me know if you'd rather extend/waive that deadline and try to work through it first before we file something.

I'll look forward to hearing from you.

Walter Sneed"

I thought it was a well-written e-mail.

Unfortunately, it was completely ineffective, because Donald Taft didn't work for Merciful anymore. So Mr. Taft didn't answer that e-mail or follow-up e-mails. Walter tried to reach him by phone, but was told by Mr. Taft's administrative assistant that Mr. Taft had retired. I was worried that Mr. Taft was let go because he was too accommodating to Walter's requests. I had a foreboding that his replacement would be more difficult to work with.

All in all, not an auspicious beginning.

Walter was informed that the attorney handling this matter would be Ann Paget, an attorney with the title "Dispute Resolution Coordinator of the Merciful Legal Division." Walter forwarded to Ann Paget the e-mail originally intended for David Taft. Ms. Paget's reply was terse:

"Thank you for your e-mail. Merciful will extend the time for you to file a Reconsideration Appeal to May 25, 2017."

Interestingly, in spite of her title, Ann Paget was not on Merciful's payroll as a staff attorney. Instead, according to the letter-head of her communications with Walter, she was employed by a six-hundred-member global law firm called Halstead and Wren LLP, which occupied a sixteen-floor building in downtown Midwest City. According to their website, Ms. Paget graduated from the University of Virginia Law School and was a partner in the firm.

Merciful had hired a big gun.

CHAPTER 8

April 2017

The first step in fighting back was to ask for reconsideration of the (cough, cough) "audit" findings. On April 25 Walter sent this letter to Ann Paget, with a copy to me:

"Dear Ms. Paget:

I am following up my conversation of April 24, 2017, with you regarding overpayment demand letters received by my client Pathology Services, PC. Today additional letters were received, which I am transmitting to you with this communication. All are incorrect."

Walter then proceeded to outline why Merciful was in the wrong. He then finished like this:

"The amount of overpayment sought thus far is approaching a million dollars. PLEASE TAKE IMMEDIATE STEPS TO ASSURE THAT RECOUPMENTS AND DENIALS DO NOT BEGIN BASED ON THIS AUDIT, because doing so could threaten the existence of Pathology Services, PC.

Sincerely,
Walter Sneed"

"Recoupments" would hold back all payments to my pathology lab from Merciful, for present and future services, until the $750,000.00 "debt" was paid. "Denials" would mean none of my bills to Merciful going forward would be paid. In summary, I would receive no money for any kind of work I did for Merciful-insured patients. Walter was not dramatizing when he said "This could threaten the existence of Pathology Services, PC." In fact, he was understating the threat. My company could not take that kind of financial hit.

It's not hard to kill a small business. A small business does not have the large footprint of a big business with lobbyists and influence, nor does it have other resources a large company has — large bank balances, lines of credit, capital, a corporate legal department, and large multinational law firms on retainer.

A trope of storytelling is that of the heroic protagonist with nothing but pluck and courage who fights an implacable evil ruthless adversary who has overwhelming resources and weapons, such that there seems to be no way the hero can win, even though he or she deserves to. In such an epic tale the hero undertakes a "hero's journey" and overcomes incredible obstacles and adversity to triumph. Of course such a story draws a large audience. Almost every film made these days has such a theme.

This book is not that story. This book is about loss of innocence.

See, I thought this was the kind of country and society where if I studied hard and went to medical school, and if I was conscientious during my internship and residency training, and if I owned a medical practice, a small business that provided a needed service — I would be rewarded. And until Merciful attacked me, I was.

I also thought that society would have some regard for its own self-interest, because not only was Pathology Services providing a benefit to me (a livelihood) and my employees, but it was also providing a benefit to patients, the hospital, and the medical community. Pathology Services provided well-qualified, well-trained pathologists and technologists who worked hard and conscientiously to provide tissue specimen interpretations and diagnoses doctors needed to take care of their patients. We were committing no crime nor selling a deleterious product. To the contrary, we were providing a good service, and I thought we were an important part of the medical community. Therefore, I did not see how it would serve anyone to try to destroy us. I never thought such a thing would happen.

But I was wrong. Merciful, and then Excel, did try to destroy me, and no one cared.

CHAPTER 9

April 2017

We quickly received an answer to our request for a reconsideration of the audit findings. The answer was "NO." The faceless but ubiquitous entity named "Provider Audit" sent this reply:

"Dear Provider:

Thank you for your recent request for reconsideration of our audit findings.

Merciful Insurance makes every effort to ensure that claims are paid correctly. Reimbursement decisions are based on document-ation you provide, nationally recognized standards of coding, Merciful Policy and Billing Guidelines, provider contracts, and Merciful Provider Administration Manuals.

This service was provided in a hospital. The pathology lab costs would have been reimbursed to the hospital. Therefore, there is no adjustment to the original findings.

If you disagree with this determination, you may file a Formal Reconsideration Appeal. This process is outlined in your Provider Administration Manual entitled Provider Dispute Resolution Procedure.

Sincerely,

Provider Audit"

Again, I felt like I was a character in Orwell's book *1984* because most of the letter was simply not true, and "Provider Audit" (how Orwellian is that!) had to know this. We did provide "documentation." We did follow "nationally recognized standards of coding," and "Merciful Policy and Billing Guidelines." There had been no changes in "provider contracts" and "Administration Manuals" for decades. It was like saying "War is peace" and "Freedom is slavery."

The statement "This service was provided in a hospital" was also a lie. "This service" was provided at my laboratory, Pathology Services, several miles from the hospital. Once again, there was a repeat of the ambiguous sentence with the phrase "would have been reimbursed to the hospital." If the money for work my pathology lab did was reimbursed to the hospital, the hospital should have passed the money to Pathology Services, which actually did the work. That didn't happen.

In summary, the letter did not convey a legitimate "reconsideration." Instead, it was a delaying tactic, the first of many. To quote Orwell again, Merciful believed "Ignorance is strength."

Of course I couldn't stop fighting. Our next step was to file a Reconsideration Appeal. Walter, Sela, and I immediately started working on that.

It's so hard for me to describe the bad guys in this story because I never met any of them, never laid eyes on them. The evildoers were faceless, nameless bureaucrats who worked in big buildings many miles away and signed their communications with monikers like "Provider Audit." What cowardice to not even sign these threatening documents! Then to defend their misdeeds, they hired an outside lawyer, Ann Paget, who worked for a large multinational legal firm. I can't describe the physical appearance of the evil persons who were taking away my livelihood because they hid their wickedness behind Merciful's corporate façade and a hired attorney.

What Merciful did to me is well described by what Hannah Arendt called "the banality of evil." I think this phrase applies to Merciful Insurance Company. It's a severe charge, but I am going to make it. Faceless, nameless, anonymous functionaries at Merciful attempted to destroy me and my company. They were not on the front lines taking care of patients and seeing the consequences of what they were trying to do to me, my business, my employees, or the patients we helped take care of. They were bureaucrats, behind the scenes, removed from the damage they did. They did these terrible things to me for no motives greater than greed and advancements of their own petty careers. Perhaps they justified their actions by thinking that if I didn't get the money I was owed for services my pathology lab did, well then, Merciful could keep costs down and lower premiums for their insured patients. They were just being efficient, trying to run a lean operation and pass on the savings to their insured patients, right?

And, dear readers, if you believe that rationale for a second, then you are even more naive than I was.

CHAPTER 10

May 2017

Merciful kept contending that "lab costs would have been reimbursed to the hospital" most recently in the missive signed by that nebulous ubiquitous entity "Provider Audit." I didn't understand what the phrase "would have been reimbursed to the hospital" meant. Was money, which should have gone to my pathology lab, paid to Excel Pinnacle Hospital or not? I needed to find out.

So I scheduled a meeting with the management of Excel Pinnacle Hospital for Tuesday, May 9 at 10 a.m. I invited the chief executive officer (CEO), chief operating officer (COO), comptroller, and laboratory manager of the hospital. Sela and I were there from Pathology Services.

I was apprehensive about the meeting. I had succeeded in the competitive field of pathology by keeping my head down and doing a good job, and not calling attention to myself or my company. Therefore, involving the management of the hospital in my problem was like a poison to me.

And I was worried about what I might find out. Maybe Merciful was paying Excel Pinnacle Hospital for work the hospital was not doing, but that Pathology Services was doing. Maybe Excel Pinnacle Hospital was keeping money that should have gone to Pathology Services. Well, that would be awkward, wouldn't it?

We met in the boardroom of the hospital. As is typical of such rooms, the room was dominated by a centrally located large oval oak table surrounded by matching oak chairs with soft tan cushions and high backs lined with dark brown leather. The wall opposite the entrance had built-in bookshelves filled with loose-leaf binders containing rules and regulations of the hospital as well as minutes of its various departments and committees – a lot of paper. The remaining walls were bright white, but broken up by official documents with black frames – Certificates of Accreditation from various entities, including Medicare, OSHA, and the Joint Commission as well as a collection of licenses from government agencies – local, federal and state. The walls looked like checkerboards. Everything the hospital did was obviously approved and supported by the healthcare licensing and accrediting agencies watching out for the interests of the public. The licenses documented that the hospital obeyed all the applicable rules, regulations, and laws of the local, state, and federal governments. Who was I to question anything?

The CEO, COO, comptroller, and laboratory manager sat on one side of the table. Sela and I sat on the other side.

The CEO, Bart Magnum, had his dark hair nicely parted on the left and combed to the right. He was dressed in a dark suit with a white shirt and solid red tie.

David Turner, the COO, was a big man, mildly overweight, who looked like a guy who had played college football as a lineman and then put on some pounds since graduation. He actually was quite athletic, but his sport in college at Midwest State University had been golf, not football. In fact, he'd even coached golf at his alma mater for a few years after he graduated, but there was more money in healthcare, so he switched to that. He was dressed in a dark suit with a white shirt and solid blue tie.

The comptroller, Brent Turner, was dressed in black trousers with suspenders, and a long-sleeved pressed 100% cotton light blue shirt, with no coat and no tie. He looked like he didn't care whether he was there or not.

The laboratory manager, Judy Rogers, was dressed in white scrubs under a white lab coat. She had a pleasant expression on her face, but had little or no interest in the topic at hand, which was anatomic pathology. Her interest was the clinical parts of the lab – chemistry, hematology, blood banking, and microbiology. The less she had to worry about tissue specimens, the better – that was *my* department. She was at the meeting as a witness sympathetic to hospital management, nothing more.

Sela wore black slacks with a red blouse and a black jacket.

And me? I was dressed in dark blue scrubs and a light blue lab coat. I looked like a sixty-eight-year-old man who woke up every morning with the aches and pains you get when you are that age. I wasn't much to look at, with only two things going for me: hair, which was gray and turning white, but still there, and weight – I weighed pretty much the same as I did when I was a varsity wrestler in high school and college.

Much of the meeting was a technical discussion regarding insurance and Medicare matters, which are arcane, confusing, and hard to understand – even for experts. I can summarize the meeting simply: I never got a straight answer from anyone at Excel Pinnacle Hospital about whether or not Merciful paid the hospital money that should have gone to Pathology Services.

The meeting started on time. I began by handing out manila folders containing the agenda for the meeting and attached pertinent documents:

Agenda

Merciful Update
May 19, 2017
Fact Finding Meeting

> 1. Report of alleged overpayment by Merciful to Pathology Services for Technical Component Services
>
>> A. Samples of Merciful Audit Demand Letters.
>> B. Time frame of asserted overpayments approximately 5/14/15–3/2/17.
>> C. Merciful contends that "it would have paid the hospital" for the pathology lab costs covered in the audit, citing Medicare rules.
>
> 2. We are preparing our response to Merciful, and we need this information:
>
>> A. Was Excel Pinnacle Hospital paid for the pathology lab costs by Merciful?

B. How does the hospital contract with Merciful differ from the hospital contract with Medicare, or are they the same?

C. Over the above time frame, has the hospital had a contract change with Merciful?

D. Have there been any communications with Merciful about reimbursements?

I then proceeded to go through the items for discussion on the agenda. Each folder had samples of the documents Merciful had sent to me, which I briefly explained. I also explained the time frame involved. Most importantly I explained that Merciful wanted back the money that they had paid me for pathology lab costs, because Merciful contended it had paid that money to the hospital.

"Is that true?" I asked. "Did Merciful Insurance Company pay Excel Pinnacle Hospital money for pathology lab costs that should have gone to Pathology Services for work that my company did?"

I thought that was a simple question. I thought wrong. You would have thought that I was asking them how much dark matter there was in the universe. Bart and David answered with nothing but facial expressions that said "Huh?"

Brent, the comptroller, said, "Merciful has various contracts with us. Some of them have been in place for twenty years or so."

"Okay," I said. "But let me ask you this: have there been any changes in those contracts in the last few years, specifically the time period of this audit that might have affected pathology lab costs reimbursement?"

"Not that I am aware of."

"Any communications about pathology lab costs?"

"Same answer."

"Any changes at all?"

"Same answer."

Silence.

Then Brent said, "We will have to investigate the applicable patient data to see what Merciful paid and what was not paid, depending on the contract."

Sela said, "I can give you examples of the various patient claims included in the audit, and I will be sure to include examples from each of the applicable contracts."

"Good," said Brent.

David, the COO, said, "I'll check with my corporate contacts and see what they know about this."

Bart Magnum asked, "How much money are we talking about?"

I said, "About three-quarters of a million dollars. Enough to put us out of business."

It was time to wrap it up. "I'll get those patient claims to you today," said Sela.

"We'll check on this stuff and get back to you, no later than a week," said Brent.

Brent did not get back to me "no later than a week." He never got back to me, ever. Sela did what she said she would do, and sent the patient/insurance information to Brent that same day. However, as I write these words, five years later, I still have not heard back from Brent or anyone else about what the contracts said, or whether or not Merciful paid pathology lab costs to the hospital. I followed up with phone calls, e-mails, and visits to pretty much every individual in the administrative suite of Excel Pinnacle Hospital, but no one ever gave me the information I needed, or gave me any indication they were working on it.

In fact, neither Excel Pinnacle Hospital nor Merciful Insurance Company ever leveled with me and gave me a straight answer to my simple question: Did Merciful pay pathology lab costs to Excel Pinnacle Hospital or not?

From Excel Pinnacle Hospital I never received any answer whatsoever. The reason for this lack of response from the hospital was that there was nothing in it for them. The amount at stake was three-quarters of a million dollars, and that was my problem. Excel Pinnacle didn't want it to be their problem.

Merciful simply asserted that they had paid the pathology lab costs to Excel Pinnacle, but never offered any documentation or proof of any kind that in fact they did so. I suspect such proof didn't exist.

There was one exception to the total silence and lack of response from Excel Pinnacle Hospital executives. David Turner, the COO, gave me a brief follow-up, and it was discouraging. A few weeks after our meeting, I encountered him as he was making rounds in the hospital. We stopped in a hospital corridor and chatted. He said, "I checked with our attorney, and we can't pay you the pathology lab costs."

"Why?" I asked.

David kind of shrugged and looked embarrassed as he said, "I guess because we're Excel, and we are big, and we can do anything we want. I hope you can work out something with Merciful."

CHAPTER 11

May 2017

To state the obvious, no one at Excel Pinnacle or Merciful cared what happened to me or Pathology Services. In a way I could understand this. I was one pathologist with little direct contact with patients. No patient was going to come to Excel Pinnacle Hospital because of its great pathology department; they were going to come to Excel Pinnacle Hospital because a great surgeon operated there, or the cardiologists of the Excel Pinnacle Hospital were highly regarded, or because of the great nursing care, or because the cafeteria food was good – not because of the pathology department.

The reasoning was similar with Merciful. No one was going to sign up with Merciful Insurance because Pathology Services was on its list of approved providers.

Also, my company was small with a small footprint and little clout. There were other pathologists, other pathology companies. What made me so special? Nothing.

Surprisingly, I was having trouble getting this concept across to Walter Sneed. During my many conversations with him, he kept using the word "partner" as in "I can't believe Merciful is treating a partner like this," or "I don't understand why the hospital isn't being more cooperative with one of its valued partners" – meaning me.

I didn't know how to respond to these statements. Was Mr. Sneed just being naïve? Hard to believe, he was an attorney, after all, and whatever negative traits lawyers might have, naivety is not one of them.

Obviously I was not regarded as Merciful's "partner." They were willing to bankrupt Pathology Services with no remorse whatsoever. And Excel Corp had no sympathy for me. I was expendable.

CHAPTER 12

May 2017

In May I got my first bill from Walter Sneed for $29,750.00, which covered the work he did in April. It was a four-page document. The first page was a summary: "Statement for Professional Services Rendered per Attached Itemization through April 30, 2017. Walter Sneed 85 hours at $350.00 per hour."

The remaining pages documented the charges and included date, billing hours (in tenths of an hour), and narrative (e.g., "telephone conversation with Jack Spenser," "letters to and from Jack Spenser," "letters to and from Sela Ray," "Preparation of Client Representation forms," "conversation with Attorney Ann Paget," "research on Medicare law," and so on).

It was depressing reading. I felt like I was in a horror movie being sucked dry by vampires. It was not only the fees that were killing me. It was also time I spent helping Walter Sneed with our legal defense. A lot of the "85 hours" of attorney time I was billed for was time Walter spent with me in person, on the phone, or via e-mails. Walter needed a lot of education from Sela and me about what the pathology lab charges entailed. Attorneys in some ways are very intelligent; they have to be because each case is a little different, and they have to be able to learn. But this pathology lab charges issue involved very obscure practices and complicated Medicare/insurance law. It was a lot of material for Walter to learn. I patiently explained to him how we handled tissue, steps involved in preparing microscopic slides, what histotechnologists did, how we issued reports, and so on. My conversations with Walter went on and on, at $350.00 an hour.

And Walter loved to have these lawyerly talks with me, which were Socratic in nature with various "riddles" – should we or should we not file a lawsuit, and should we or should we not go to arbitration? Walter discussed these issues in eloquent ways that I'm sure were quite wise and profound. But nothing was ever resolved, and these meetings took time – time away from my main job, which was taking care of patients.

I was getting hit financially in two ways. First, I had legal expenses. Second, money coming to Pathology Services was decreasing because I was not getting paid for pathology lab charges by Merciful. I was not bringing in enough money to meet expenses, including meeting a payroll of twenty employees every month. Twenty families were counting on that. The situation was this: not only did I not have enough income to make a profit; I didn't have enough money to stay in business.

CHAPTER 13

May 2017

The stakes weren't just financial. Even if I could survive the financial hit from Merciful (which I could not) – providing free pathology lab services to Merciful-insured patients was (and is) against the law. If I accepted such a situation, I would be breaking anti-kickback laws, RICO laws, and finally a law regarding physician referrals called the Stark law. I could go to jail.

So why didn't I just quit? I mean, I was sixty-eight years old, certainly old enough to retire. I didn't need any more money, and I certainly didn't need the hassles of a stressful pathology practice and the liability of running a business, for which I got no appreciation from Merciful or Excel Pinnacle. Appreciation!? I didn't even get cooperation, like paying for the three-quarters of a million dollars of pathology lab charges for work we had already performed. Why didn't I just close Pathology Services, lock the doors, and head off into the sunset?

I couldn't.

See, this wasn't an antique store I was running, where I could just sell off the inventory, square things away with the landlord, pay the employees what I owed, and leave. And it wasn't like I owned a factory making coat hangers, where I would have to do something about the machines and equipment, and clean up any messes the factory made, but with relatively little hassle, I could exit the business. And I wasn't a clinician leaving a practice, like a surgeon or a pediatrician or an internist. Such a practitioner has much less equipment than my pathology lab did and, more importantly, does not have to store tissue specimens from patients, like my pathology lab did. The only tangible things a clinician possesses are the patients' medical records. A clinical specialist could bring in a partner to take over the practice, or sell the practice to another practitioner, and walk away. And even if the practice is closed completely, it is relatively easy to get the medical records to the patients themselves (if they want them) or the physician taking over their care.

Closing down Pathology Services, however, would be different and much more difficult. In fact, it would be impossible. Not only did my pathology lab have inventory, equipment, employees, and patient records – but it had microscopic slides and tissue representing over 200,000 specimens from thousands of patients. This repository of specimens was used for ongoing patient care. For example, suppose a patient has a brain tumor, incurable, but a new drug comes along that works really well against brain tumors: there's a catch though – to determine whether this drug is effective for this particular patient, it has to be tested on the patient's brain tumor tissue located in my lab. If I closed Pathology Services and walked away, that brain tumor tissue would not be available for such testing. I daresay the patient and the patient's family would be very angry at me that this option for good treatment was not available. We received over a dozen requests for such testing every day. New treatment options become available quite often, and new tests are needed to be performed on the tissue samples stored in Pathology Services Laboratory. If I deserted my pathology lab and locked the doors, I would be making unavailable all those slides and tissues from thousands of patients, as well as the associated patient records. That would have severe repercussions.

So closing Pathology Services would not really work for me unless I wanted to defend myself against countless lawsuits by irate patients. In addition there were medical licensing boards, laboratory accrediting agencies, and other authorities who were monitoring me to make sure I took good care of the patients in our state. Their enforcement divisions would be very unhappy if I just abandoned my lab. At a minimum, I would lose my medical license for such negligence. Hell, they might even regard Pathology Services as criminally reckless and prosecute the person responsible (me). I think a judge and jury would have much more sympathy for the patients who were harmed than for me. At the very least, I would be fined a lot of money. I might even lose my freedom.

So closing Pathology Services and walking away was not an option.

In summary, if I kept Pathology Services open, I would probably go to jail for violating various kickback laws. And if I closed Pathology Services, I would be recklessly endangering patients and risk severe punishments.

Could I sell Pathology Services and walk away and let someone else worry about closing it or keeping open? No. Anyone who bought my company would have the same problems I had, and with a $750,000.00 liability to Merciful. No one in their right mind would buy my company.

I saw no way out of my predicament. I felt like a rat in a maze with no exit and no solution and no options. It was very depressing. I contemplated suicide. Things were that grim. The only sane response was to panic.

And to fight.

CHAPTER 14

May 2017

Walter asked me, "Are you familiar with any other independent pathology labs like yours that are getting similar letters from Merciful?"

I was not. As far as I knew, I was the only one unfortunate enough to be targeted by these "audits." There were a couple of reasons for this.

First, many pathologists in the state were employed by hospitals and therefore weren't receiving pathology lab cost payments from insurance companies or other payers. Merciful was not paying these pathology lab costs to these pathologists because the hospitals were supplying the pathology lab services with their own laboratories. Therefore, such pathologists weren't getting hassled by Merciful because they weren't receiving money from Merciful; they never had.

Second, the several pathology groups in the state that were not part of a hospital and had independent labs like me, well, they were my competitors. So none of my competitors would help me by relating to me information about their relationships with Merciful Insurance. They would be thrilled if Pathology Services went out of business and the pathology contract at Excel Pinnacle Hospital was available. Other pathology groups in the state would swoop in with offers to take over the hospital pathology contract as rapidly as humanly possible. My bad luck would be their opportunity. Pathology was a cutthroat business.

The most cutthroat of all was my main competitor, Federated Pathologists. Federated Pathologists had the same business model as I did. The difference was this: Federated was by far the biggest pathology company in the state, or the Midwest; it was a five-hundred-million-dollar-revenue company with over a hundred pathologists. I was a five-million-dollar company with three pathologists. Federated had contracts with over a hundred hospitals throughout the country, not just in this state. I had a contract with one hospital. Finally, Federated not only had pathology lab services, but had clinical pathology operations as well, which did chemistry, hematology, and microbiology testing – none of which Pathology Services provided. They even did transfusion medicine. At Pathology Services we were an anatomic pathology operation only.

The difference in our two companies was important. It meant that even if Merciful was refusing to pay Federated for the pathology lab costs of processing tissue, Federated could make up the shortfall in other areas, like their clinical pathology operations – chemistry, hematology, microbiology, and transfusion medicine – which were quite lucrative. Or they could make it up with income from other states where insurance companies were paying their charges without the hassles that Merciful was causing in Midwest State. In summary, the anatomic pathology lab part of Federated's operation just wasn't that big a deal to Federated. But it was a big deal to me; that's all I had.

Or Merciful might not even attack Federated in the first place because of the resources a five-hundred-million-dollar company would have that I did not have.

Or even if Merciful did attack Federated and withhold payments from Federated, here is the way I think Federated would react: Federated would live with the situation, at least for a while, thinking that Merciful would eventually "see the light," recognize the error of their ways, and reinstate the payments to Federated – AFTER their other competitors, like me, were put out of business. Then Federated could swoop in and pick up the pieces. Federated would be thrilled if I went bankrupt so that they could replace me at Excel Pinnacle Hospital. In fact, Federated would happily help the process along.

CHAPTER 15

May 2017

An important part of our fight against Merciful was to submit an "Audit Reconsideration Appeal," which we did at 5 p.m. on May 25, 2017, right at the deadline. Walter sent it to Ann Paget by e-mail, with a copy to me. It was a long document (fourteen pages), and a lot of it was written in legalese. Nevertheless, Walter eloquently made these points:

1. Merciful was retroactively applying a policy after Pathology Services did the work.

2. Merciful's request for recoupment funds was based solely on <u>Medicare</u> policy, not applicable to Merciful.

3. There was nothing in my contract with Merciful whatsoever that adopted Medicare policy for Merciful-insured patients, nor was there any notice that such a policy had been adopted, and finally there was no notice that such a policy would be adopted.

4. The "audit" statement that the pathology lab services were "provided by the hospital" and "would have been reimbursed to the hospital" was incorrect. First, this work was provided by Pathology Services, not the hospital. Second, the statement "would have been paid to the hospital" was ambiguous. The "audit" did not document any such payment to the hospital, and the hospital has not notified Pathology Services of any such payment. If in fact Merciful paid the hospital for work Pathology Services did, then obviously the overpayment letters and

recoupment efforts should have been directed to the hospital, not Pathology Services.

5. Merciful gave no notice whatsoever of a change in reimbursement. Of note, Merciful could have prospectively asked Pathology Services to provide such services, without Merciful paying for such services, but only with advance notice. That would have given Pathology Services the right to refuse to provide the service, or make arrangements with the hospital to get paid the money that Merciful contended it paid to the hospital. But Merciful did not give such notice before the refund demands.

I was impressed with Walter's writing. He made a convincing case. What he presented in the appeal were facts, not "my side of the story." Everything he wrote was true.

Merciful had thirty days to send us a response.

CHAPTER 16

June 2017

I received an invoice from Mr. Sneed for his services during May for $38,150.00. I felt like Pathology Services was a carcass getting picked at by a couple of vultures, Merciful and Walter's law firm.

What really galled me was that Walter attached a note to the invoice that said, "I hope this compares favorably with the 'big firm' lawyer."

Are you kidding me?! My initial thought was to reply that if this kind of favorable legal representation continued much longer, Pathology Services would be bankrupt. Instead, I sent an e-mail that simply said "So far Merciful owes my company $79,000.00 for unpaid charges." I know I sounded ungrateful for Walter's efforts, but this arrogance in the absence of tangible results was driving me nuts.

The bills were itemized, noting what Walter did and the time involved. They were maddening, all this work with so little results. Of course, much of Walter's time was spent talking to me on the phone. My conversations with Walter were frustrating. I had to continue to educate Walter about our pathology business, which was necessary and worth the time, trouble, and expense. But many of Walter's phone calls were not all that productive. For example, Walter and I spent an inordinate amount of time discussing our various options – getting an injunction, filing a lawsuit, seeking arbitration...but I couldn't get Walter to make decisions about what to actually *do*. But the lack of decisions didn't stop Walter from writing drafts of injunctions, lawsuits, and arbitration proposals – then sending the bills to me for the time he spent drafting these documents. The billable hours went up. Walter sent me drafts of these documents, and they were very lawyerly and eloquent. Walter was an excellent writer.

I approved the lawsuits, arbitration requests, injunctions, and other actions – in writing. I signed the affidavits, and Sela notarized them. I asked Walter to move forward with these legal maneuvers as soon as possible, and to file a lawsuit and injunction immediately. There was no time to waste. I was running out of money fast.

THEN NOTHING HAPPENED.

Walter had these great documents on his desk, written and approved by me, which he refused to actually file with the court. He was like General McClellan with his large well-trained Army of the Potomac, which he refused to let fight in a battle. The lawsuit in particular was a winner, in my opinion. But Walter would not file it. I asked, "Why?" I asked that several times.

And I got several answers. "Merciful was big and Pathology Services was small," and "If you file a lawsuit against Merciful, they will fight back hard; they will show no mercy," and "Be careful about waking a sleeping dragon," and "If you come for the king, you'd best not miss."

Basically, Walter contended that if I filed the lawsuit, Merciful would use every legal maneuver available to fight it. Walter sent me some documentation about a lawsuit involving a group of ER doctors who filed a lawsuit against Merciful, and the extreme measures Merciful took to defend itself and win. Walter said, "If we file this lawsuit, Merciful will fight it to the death, your death."

What I could not get across to Walter was that my company was already dying, and I had nothing left to lose. If Pathology Services didn't get reimbursed for our pathology lab charges to Merciful, my company was dead anyway. At least I wanted to go down fighting. But Walter *would not* file the lawsuit or the injunction or anything else with any court anywhere. I wondered, was Walter afraid of Merciful?

Walter also was spending what I regarded as an inordinate amount of time on the phone talking with Ann Paget, the attorney for Merciful, which of course was more billable time for Walter and his firm. Walter described these calls as "productive" or "fruitful" or "helpful" or "promising." But then again, NOTHING HAPPENED – no settlement, no halt to the recoupments, no response to our appeal, or any other tangible progress. Just more legal bills, sometimes with the comment about how much better he was doing for me than "those big city lawyers out east would do." Maddening.

The month of June started with a huge setback. Merciful began taking back (recouping) the money it contended my company, Pathology Services, owed them. Simply put, Merciful stopped paying Pathology Services any money whatsoever. Merciful stopped paying the pathology lab costs, of course, but also stopped paying the professional fees I and my employee pathologists submitted for examining the specimens sent to us. Merciful stopped all payments to my company and planned to do so until we worked off the approximately $750,000.00 Merciful contended it was owed. In summary, Merciful said: YOU GET NOTHING.

Merciful was my largest payer; 35% of my revenues came from Merciful. Obviously when Merciful stopped paying my company any money at all, my revenues went down 35%. There went any profit my company might have and then some. And Merciful would continue not paying Pathology Services until it worked off the $750,000.00 the "audit" said we owed.

But there was no guarantee my nightmare would end, even then. Years down the line, after my company provided three-quarters of a million dollars of work of unreimbursed work for Merciful-insured patients, Merciful could then decide to do another "audit" and find another way not to pay me and my company for the work we did. For example, another "audit" could retrospectively conclude that not only pathology lab costs, but the money Merciful had paid to me and my pathologist colleagues for the professional services of examining specimens and rendering diagnoses and interpretations – well, that was also included in the "bundled payments" to the hospital too; therefore, I had to return those payments as well. What was going to stop them from doing that? Nothing. An indentured servant would get a better deal. Again, I felt like I was a character in a Kafka novel. This couldn't be real life.

And here's the catch. I could not simply tell Merciful to shove it, and refuse to provide pathology services to Merciful-insured patients. If a Merciful-insured patient came to Excel Pinnacle Hospital and needed an operation or some sort of tissue study, that specimen was sent to Pathology Services, and it was my job to examine, process, interpret and diagnose all such specimens – regardless of the insurance status of the patient or ability to pay. I had to. This language was in the contract my company had with the hospital. It was also the law of the land because of anti-dumping regulations and other rules. I couldn't refuse to provide needed care, i.e., pathology services, to any patient just because I didn't get paid for that service. If Merciful didn't pay my company for the work we did, well, that was my problem.

Merciful stopped paying Pathology Services in spite of the fact that we had not heard back anything about our Reconsideration/Appeal, and in spite of Walter's communication to Ann Paget on April 25, 2017, which included the statement/request that recoupments and denials not begin based on the "audit."

I phoned Walter immediately and told him that the recoupments and denials had begun, and that Merciful was not paying me anything.

Walter said, "I was afraid this would happen."

To his credit, Walter did understand the urgency of the matter. He phoned Ann Paget immediately and asked that Merciful stop the recoupments at once. She said that "stopping recoupments is not our usual practice."

On June 6, Walter sent this e-mail to Ann Paget, with a copy to me:

"A month ago I requested any communication that changed the contractual agreement between Merciful and Pathology Services. There is not one mentioned in the 'audit,' and nothing was provided to answer my request thirty days ago. If there is something, it should not be that hard to produce. If the audit is in error, which I believe it is, then undoing the recoupments will be a logistical nightmare as well as a cash flow issue. Undoing recoupments will be a struggle for both sides. If Merciful can't provide you with a written commun-ication by tomorrow, holding off the recoupment at least for a while would seem to make sense for both sides, regardless of what Merciful's usual practice is."

Walter phoned me a short time after I received the e-mail and said that he and Ann Paget had a phone call meeting set up for the next day at 3 p.m.

My company would go out of business quickly if Merciful continued to withhold all payments to me and my company, regardless of the justice of my cause. Without such payments I wouldn't be able to continue to fight. And even if I won, it would be too late. Without money to pay employees, pay the bills, and keep the business running – Pathology Services would cease to operate and close its doors. And there would be no way to get it back. The employees would get other jobs. The equipment and computers would eventually be useless. Pathology Services would be gone by the time Merciful eventually paid me the money they owed me.

CHAPTER 17

June 2017

Walter's phone call on June 7 with Ann Paget went well. Merciful consented to our request to stop recoupments, and to start paying my bills. Walter phoned me with the good news. Walter said that Merciful agreed to "a short tolling of recoupment for thirty days," which I understood to mean that the recoupments would stop for thirty days, which meant Merciful would start paying me again, at least for thirty days. Finally, a victory!

I thought this was good news for three reasons.

First, stopping the recoupments for thirty days meant that for the next thirty days Merciful would pay my company's charges, and thus I could survive for at least thirty days. The tolling agreement was set to last from June 8, 2017, to July 8, 2017. Merciful was apparently willing to put everything "on hold" until they responded to our Reconsideration Appeal. Merciful's response was due in late June.

Second, I found it very interesting and hopeful that Merciful was willing to stop their recoupment efforts, even if only for a little while, because to quote Ms. Paget "stopping recoupment is not our usual practice." Since they were not following their usual practice, I suspected that Merciful knew that this whole "audit" scam was wrong and would not withstand any scrutiny, e.g., a lawsuit or arbitration.

Third, halting the recoupment efforts told me that Merciful's legal team was willing to be reasonable.

CHAPTER 18

June 2017

On June 9, I received this e-mail from Walter with some attachments:

"Here's a copy of signed documents halting the recoupments. I think to some extent they did this as special treatment, perhaps due to my history with Merciful."

I continued to be amazed at Walter's insecurities. He had to build himself up with a comment like "special treatment perhaps due to my history with Merciful."

Maybe. But my thinking was that Merciful knew that what they were doing was out of line, and that if this case was ever presented to an arbitration panel, a jury, or a judge – they would lose big time. So Merciful backed off, at least a little.

But only a little. Ms. Paget's communication to Walter also had some bad news. She said in the e-mail to him: "Merciful is reviewing the Reconsideration Appeal submitted by your client and will provide a response. In the meantime, Pathology Services should review the audit and follow the guidance to avoid future denial of payments for the same reason."

That comment told me two things. First, our Reconsideration Appeal would be denied. Second, that in the long run my cause was hopeless. Even if I prevailed in arbitration or a lawsuit and the retrospective findings of the audit were overturned, Merciful would simply apply the "guidance" going forward and deny payments for the pathology lab costs going forward. I would be presented with an amended contract or a new contract, which would explicitly deny any such payments, and there wouldn't be a darn thing I could do about it.

The arbitration procedure was covered in my contract with Merciful. It was relatively simple. The arbitration panel would be composed of three individuals – one chosen by Merciful, one chosen by me, and those two would choose the third member. The arbitration panel would listen to arguments and evidence from both sides and make a recommendation. There was no doubt in my mind the arbitration panel would decide in my favor.

Or I could sue. Again, I was confident I would win a lawsuit at trial.

But I wasn't sure that winning an arbitration and/or lawsuit would help me that much. The arbitration process would take time – time to appoint and agree on arbitrators, to prepare a presentation, schedule the meeting, and wait for a decision...

And a lawsuit would take even more time with delays due to discovery and its associated interrogatories and depositions. If I filed a lawsuit, Merciful would slow the process as much as possible with continuances and other delays. A lawsuit would take years to get resolved, either by trial or settlement.

By the time the matter was resolved, either by arbitration or litigation, sometime in the distant future, Pathology Services would be long gone, destroyed by lack of income and legal fees. Winning would be irrelevant, and Merciful knew it.

CHAPTER 19

June 2017

I was anxious to hear Merciful's response to our Reconsideration /Appeal, which we filed in late May. Merciful had thirty days to respond. As each day in June went by, I became more and more impatient. I so much wanted to get this dispute with Merciful resolved, and the response of Merciful to our Appeal was an important part of that process. I didn't see how in the world they would defend what they were doing, because, well, it was indefensible.

Finally, in the late afternoon of the thirtieth day since they received our Audit Reconsideration/ Appeal, Merciful finally sent their Response – at the last minute of the last possible day.

It wasn't a very long document. If I wrote it, I would be embarrassed. If the matter weren't so serious, I would have thought their response was a joke. If Merciful's arguments went before an arbitration panel or a judge or a jury – they would be laughed at. But I wasn't laughing. The following was Merciful's Response, with my comments in italics:

The first page simply defined various terms.

We already knew all that.

Next the Response declared that Merciful's contract with the hospital described an "all-inclusive rate," which covered the pathology lab costs my company, Pathology Services, was submitting to Merciful.

This was the toughest part of the Response to refute – first, because "all-inclusive rate" was such an ambiguous phrase, and second, Walter and I had no access to the contracts between Merciful and Excel Pinnacle Hospital. We had no idea whether the "all-inclusive rate" included my money or not. But we did know this: Excel Pinnacle Hospital was not passing on any funds whatsoever to me or my company.

Moving on…The Response then referred to the Merciful Provider Manual, which outlined how Pathology Services was to bill Merciful for our services to Merciful-insured patients.

This is exactly what we did. Merciful didn't even contend that our bills were in error, e.g., that my company billed for services that were not done or that our billing methodology was incorrect.

Then the Response veered from the ambiguous and irrelevant to the surreal. It said "Merciful pays for pathology lab services under methodologies created by Medicare. Merciful follows Medicare guidelines in determining which services are considered hospital services that are part of the payments to hospitals."

*This reasoning was flawed. First, the "methodologies created by Medicare" applied only to Medicare, a government program, and had nothing to do with private health insurance companies like United, Cigna, Aetna, Blue Cross/Blue Shield…or **Merciful**. Second, the "methodologies created by Medicare" included payments to me from the hospital for the pathology lab costs. In fact, this happened and was happening; my company **did** get reimbursed the pathology lab costs from the hospital for **Medicare** patients only. My company **did not** get such reimbursement for **Merciful** patients. An important distinction! Medicare didn't expect my pathology lab to give away the services for free. Merciful did.*

A list of what was not addressed in the Response would fill a long book, but the most significant absence was this: There was no documentation of any change in the business relationship of Merciful with Pathology Services, which had included paying me the pathology lab services for decades. The response had no references to contract changes, new clauses, notifications, clarifications… nothing – *because there weren't any.* Merciful out of the blue decided not to pay me for work my company did and was doing. There was no rationale, no documentation…nothing. It was coercion.

In summary, I thought that the Response of Merciful to our Reconsideration/Appeal was very weak. Of course, Walter agreed with that opinion, but then he got paid to agree with our side and to keep fighting.

My perception, though, was that even Merciful's lawyer, Ann Paget, thought that this Response would not hold up to scrutiny. Ms. Paget closed the Response in this way: "Merciful is willing to engage in dialogue to try to resolve this matter. To that end Merciful agrees to stop further recoupment to allow the parties to work toward resolution of this matter. Merciful looks forward to continuing these discussions after your review of this Response."

In other words, until this matter was resolved, Merciful would pay my bills – an important concession to say the least. This part of the Response was kind of conciliatory, I thought. And hopeful. My impression was that Ann Paget knew, and Merciful knew, that their case was a weak one, and that they did not want this matter to go to arbitration or litigation, because they would lose. A loss was the last thing Merciful wanted. For years Merciful had bullied physicians and hospitals into accepting less money for services to Merciful-insured patients. It was so bad that it was hard for these providers to make a profit. Merciful could call the shots, because Merciful was the biggest insurer in the state and had a four-billion-dollar war chest to fight anyone who didn't cave in. But if I fought back and won, other providers might consider taking on mighty Merciful in their disputes. Merciful sure didn't want that, so I thought there was a good chance Merciful would want to settle this case and make the whole thing go away.

CHAPTER 20

June 2017

Walter Sneed tried to contact Carey Larkin, the attorney for Excel Hospital Corporation, to try to determine whether Excel Pinnacle Hospital was in fact receiving pathology lab reimbursements, something I had been unsuccessful in finding out.

Walter was unsuccessful as well. Carey Larkin didn't return his phone calls or e-mails. It was total silence. Like everyone at Excel, she was not eager to help us.

Well, Ms. Larkin could run, but she could not hide. At the Excel Pinnacle medical staff meeting in June, she was scheduled to make a presentation to the doctors about how to transfer patients from the Excel Pinnacle emergency room to other hospitals in ways that complied with the laws covering the process, the "anti-dumping" statutes. As a pathologist, I never transferred any patients anywhere, so the topic had nothing to do with me. Nevertheless, I was sure to be at that medical staff meeting. I wanted to meet Carey Larkin and talk to her.

So there I was at the June medical staff meeting, and I tried to pay attention to her talk about how to legally transfer patients from the emergency room at Excel Pinnacle Hospital to another hospital, and how to stay out of trouble with the authorities. For me it was a pretty boring topic, because it didn't apply to anything I ever did. Nevertheless, I couldn't help but pay attention, because she was a good speaker who made the topic quite interesting. She was an attractive woman, in her fifties, with blond hair. Her most striking feature, however, was her height. She was over six feet tall and very athletic looking and very fit, like one of those bicycle enthusiasts you see pedaling away on the bicycle paths that are cropping up all over the place. After she completed her presentation and the medical staff meeting was concluded, I walked over to her and introduced myself.

Then I said, "I know Walter Sneed has contacted you on my behalf about the pathology lab cost reimbursements that Merciful is not paying me."

Ms. Larkin said, "Yes, I know. What Merciful is doing is very bad."

"Any help you can give me would be appreciated."

"Well, we are doing what we can. Merciful is not just doing this to you, but doing the same thing to other groups like Federated. Hospitals across the state are dealing with the same issue. We are working with the Midwest State Hospital Association to make it quite clear that what Merciful is doing, withholding funds that are supposed to go to the pathologists – it's unacceptable."

She was many inches taller than I was, so I was looking up. I said, "I appreciate that. But this is what I really need: When my fight with Merciful is resolved, I suspect that going forward, Merciful will not pay me for the pathology lab costs. I know you have a lot of contracts with my competitor, Federated Laboratories, and my understanding is that you are paying Federated the pathology lab costs for Merciful-insured patients who come to Excel Hospitals. I am asking you that when Merciful stops paying the pathology lab costs to my company, Pathology Services, that Excel pay my company the same rate for pathology lab costs that you are paying Federated."

Carey Larkin said, "We are not paying any money to Federated."

I shook my head in disbelief. "You're not?"

"No."

CHAPTER 21

June 2017

I sent an e-mail to Walter describing my conversation with Carey Larkin. He responded with this e-mail:

"I need to pin down with Carey Larkin, the hospital attorney, whether or not Excel Pinnacle Hospital is getting paid for pathology lab costs, since Merciful has not shared with us any documentation that such is the case. I also need to discuss with her why they think they don't have to pay you. I cannot exclude the possibility that they may consider contracting with another pathology group that would do the work for free."

I sent Walter this e-mail:

"Absolutely they are considering contracting with another group, like Federated. Pathology is a very competitive field. The CEO of Excel Pinnacle Hospital gets every offer imaginable to switch from us to another vendor. If this fight with Merciful is not resolved soon, I won't have a contract, and I won't have a business."

Walter answered:

"That is exactly the point of my attack. Merciful has created a situation that foreseeably results in violation of the federal anti-kickback law. I don't have a silver bullet for your dilemma, which seems to me to be a potential violation of federal law, and going unpaid to boot, OR making so much noise that you are out of a job, OR becoming a whistleblower that could be monetarily advantageous to you in your retirement.

"I think there is evidence that what Merciful is doing fits within a criminal statute. I think our approach has some chance of success. I would not rule out the possibility that my discussions with Ann

Paget may be prompting some internal actions within Merciful. As you have pointed out, they are being more helpful than they have to be – continuing to pay you, having discussions to resolve the matter, and getting us the information that we request."

CHAPTER 22

June 2017

What Merciful and Excel were doing to me was illegal. So Walter wanted me to be a whistleblower because it was likely that other pathologists and laboratories in the state (e.g., Federated) were also not getting paid the money that they were owed for pathology lab services (which was what Carey Larkin told me). To that end Walter wanted me to talk to an attorney in Midwest City who did that kind of whistleblower work and would help me take this information to the authorities at the United States Attorney's Office, the inspector general of Medicare, the FBI, and anyone else who would be interested in prosecuting these lawbreakers.

I had no interest in being a whistleblower for these reasons:

1. Being a whistleblower would end my career as a pathologist. No one would want to hire me or do business with a whistleblower, a tattletale.

2. Instead of being a pathologist, I would be part of a team of attorneys, law enforcement officers, and government bureaucrats who would "go after" Merciful Insurance Company and Excel Hospital Corporation. I would spend a significant part of my "golden years" talking to these individuals in law offices, conference rooms, and courts of law. The logistics alone would drive me crazy – traveling to Midwest City to meet with these people, trying to find the right building, looking for a place to park my car, and working with people I probably wouldn't like very much. Also, Merciful and Excel Corp would fight back, which meant I would have to help answer interrogatories, give

depositions, and possibly testify at a trial. Merciful and Excel Corp certainly deserved any bad things that happened to them, including significant fines or even jail time, but I really didn't want to get involved in all that stuff. I just wanted to be left alone to do my job as a pathologist.

3. There was no guarantee that I would be on the winning side. My experience with lawsuits is that predicting the outcome is impossible. My first rule of lawsuits is that no one knows anything. Merciful and Excel would be formidable adversaries. My side would be up against very clever executives and attorneys.

4. I wasn't sure that anyone – the Medicare inspector general, United States Attorney, Justice Department personnel, FBI agents, a judge, members of a jury, or anyone else would care about pathologists and whether we got paid the money we were owed, or that we were harmed by organizations breaking the law. Sadly, my experience is that no one is concerned about the welfare of pathologists. Pathologists have direct contact with specimens, not patients. Few people know what pathologists do, and virtually none care. I think the authorities would be more interested in pursuing wrongdoing if surgeons, internists, pediatricians, or ob-gyn doctors were the victims. For example, if I were a pediatrician with my own practice, bearing the costs of running the business, and I was vaccinating young kids against serious disease, do you think for a minute Excel and Merciful would do to a pediatrician what they did to me – i.e., stop reimbursing the pediatrician for the vaccine supply, and retrospectively demanding reimbursements of previous payments via an "audit"? Or do such a thing to other pediatricians in the state? Rhetorical questions. Merciful and Excel wouldn't dare because pediatricians are targets who would elicit sympathy. Merciful and Excel would be asked: "How could you do such a thing to the children of our state?" Bad look. In contrast, not many persons would care about what happened to pathologists looking at specimens.

CHAPTER 23

June 2017

As far as I could tell, the situation with Merciful was hopeless. Merciful had turned down our appeal, and soon the recoupments would start again. I was losing money, taking on all the liability of owning a business and practicing medicine, with none of the benefits. And no one cared, not Merciful, not Excel Pinnacle, no one. I couldn't sell the company. No one would buy a business that was losing money. I couldn't continue on under the present conditions. I didn't want to be a whistleblower. The demand letters resulting from Merciful's "audit" began arriving in April, and almost three months later in late June there was no resolution in sight. I could not get across to Walter the urgency of the situation.

All things considered, I thought the bankruptcy of Pathology Services, PC, was the best option. I could walk away, and someone else, perhaps a bankruptcy court judge, could negotiate with Merciful. Someone else could close down the company and deal with the microscopic slides, paraffin blocks, and other patient materials. Good luck with that. I was through, totally burnt out.

I brought up the bankruptcy idea with Walter. Not surprisingly, he was totally unenthusiastic about that option. Walter continued to think that we would prevail if I would just stay the course. He didn't understand that while he was writing an elegant appeal that was rejected, and composing lawsuits and injunctions that didn't get filed with a court – I was trying to run a business and meet a payroll under duress. Merciful would soon stop paying Pathology Services again, and when that happened, I would have limited resources to keep the company running let alone continue the fight with Merciful. Based on what had happened so far, by the time Walter delivered his promised victory, my company would be broke with no employees and no business. I was not seeing any grounds for optimism.

So I phoned Raymond Scott, the attorney we had on retainer, and discussed the idea of bankruptcy with him. He wasn't any more enthusiastic about the idea of bankruptcy than Walter was.

"Jack," he said, "if you go the bankruptcy route, you're not gonna like it. You will be assigned a bankruptcy judge, who will take over the running of your company, and you won't be able to do anything without the judge's approval. And I know you don't like other people telling you what to do. I do not advise you to do this."

Nevertheless, Raymond gave me the name of the law firm he regarded as the best in bankruptcy law, a very specialized field. It was a father-son practice, Levine and Levine, and their office was in downtown Midwest City. I made an appointment to see them. I scheduled the meeting at a time when both Sela and Raymond could attend, a 9 a.m. meeting in a few days.

Sela and I drove to the meeting together. We left early to allow plenty of time to get there, because Midwest City traffic is unpredictable, and you never know how long it will take to find a place to park. We were lucky. Traffic wasn't bad, and we found a parking place with plenty of open spaces. Raymond Scott's office was also in downtown Midwest City, within easy walking distance to where we were meeting, so he would meet us at the offices of Levine and Levine.

Sela and I enjoyed the walk to the law offices. It was early morning, so the summer Midwest City heat hadn't quite yet arrived. On the way we passed a small city park with grass, a few trees, and a couple of benches. Other than that, it was all skyscrapers and sidewalks.

Sela and I arrived about thirty minutes early, but that was okay because Steven Levine was ready to see us. He came to meet us in the reception area. In this father-son firm, Steven was obviously the father. He was around my age, late sixties to early seventies. Mr. Levine was a short rotund man with gray hair combed straight back. He was dressed in a dark suit, white shirt, and striped red and black bowtie. He seemed to be a cheerful man with a ready jovial jocular smile and an apparent attitude of what a crazy world it is that we live in, but we might as well enjoy it.

The three of us took an elevator down a few floors to a conference room with no windows. Like most conference rooms, it was dominated by a centrally located large oval wooden table. Actually, the table more than dominated; there wasn't much of anything else in the room.

While we waited for Raymond Scott, I started to tell Mr. Levine my story about what Merciful was doing to me. About halfway through my recital, Raymond joined us.

Steve Levine was not only a bankruptcy attorney, but also owned and operated some nursing homes. Therefore, he was very familiar with the shenanigans of insurance companies and smiled knowingly as I told my tale. He agreed with me that what Merciful was doing was an overreach and would not stand up to scrutiny. He said, "Merciful does not want this to go to arbitration. They will lose, and there will be a record of them losing, which would be a precedent. They will do everything they can to avoid arbitration."

That was encouraging, but I had kind of figured that out already: Merciful's strategy was to string me along and wear me out.

Mr. Levine continued, "I don't think bankruptcy will help you. How old are you?"

"Just turned sixty-eight."

"Instead of bankruptcy, I recommend that you sell your company. Retire."

Raymond said, "Selling your company will solve 95% of your problems."

CHAPTER 24

June 2017

It was easy for Steve Levine and Raymond Scott to recommend selling my company, but who would want to buy it with a pending $750,000.00 hit from Merciful? I had to get rid of that debt before I could sell the company or do anything else. I thought we would win an arbitration hearing, but Mr. Levine was right – Merciful would delay the arbitration as long as possible. In fact, that was already happening. Whenever Walter asked for names of potential arbitrators from Ann Paget, her response was always the same – that she "was working on it." She had been "working on it" for several weeks with no progress. Because of these delaying tactics, I thought Walter and I should skip the arbitration.

The best option I saw was filing a lawsuit against Merciful, which would include an injunction so my business could stay open while the lawsuit was decided. Walter had prepared just such a lawsuit, which was well written. He was a better writer than lawyer. The first several pages of it detailed the same points we had made in the appeal. Then Walter finished the lawsuit this way:

Pathology Services seeks the following:

1. A temporary restraining order preventing the withholding of payments due to Pathology Services for present services, to prevent immediate and irreparable injury, loss, and damage to Pathology Services as a result of violation of its rights, in that Merciful's actions will make a final judgment ineffectual.

2. Monetary judgment for

a. Breach of contract
b. All amounts of money which Merciful has wrongfully deducted from revenues that were payable to Pathology Services
c. For treble damages resulting from diversion of funds by Merciful for money properly payable to Pathology Services
d. For violation of Merciful's obligations under Midwest State Code Ann. Section 56.7-109
e. For damages and 25% penalty under Midwest Code Ann. 56.7-105
f. For violation of the Consumer Protection Act
g. For interest, costs, and attorneys' fees
h. For such other violations and damages as may be shown at the conclusion of this matter

Respectfully submitted,

Walter L. Sneed

I thought the lawsuit was a winner. I was ticked off and wanted the lawsuit filed as soon as possible. Walter wanted my approval in writing, which I did via a notarized statement.

And then again, NOTHING HAPPENED. I could not get Walter to file the darn thing. He gave me every excuse imaginable. Here is a sample: "You can't be like a bull in a china shop – a lawsuit may cause enough damage to your company that you can't sell it, i.e., you broke all the merchandise. For example, if you file this lawsuit, it may affect your contract with Merciful such that they drop you as a provider, which would mean you couldn't take care of Merciful-insured patients that go to Excel Pinnacle, which means you would lose the hospital contract."

Walter also said, "Merciful will fight a lawsuit. You will awaken a dragon. Merciful is huge and will use its resources to fight you. They will kick you off all their insurance plans. They will use technicalities in ERISA law to counter your arguments, like saying you are refusing to provide benefits as required by law. They will bury you with interrogatories, depositions, continuances and other time-consuming maneuvers. Merciful has unlimited firepower, and we do not."

What I could not get across to Walter was that even if what he was saying had merit, I had nothing to lose. I could not get across to Walter the urgency of the situation (and maybe he didn't care as long as I was paying his invoices). My company could not survive very long under the present conditions. Pathology Services was hemorrhaging money with expenses, including a payroll that supported twenty families, bills for supplies, rent, and last but not least, lawyer bills. I knew that filing a lawsuit would tick off Merciful, and that they would fight with delaying tactics to the point that even if I won, it would be too late. And that was if Merciful fought me legally, which was no sure thing. It was obvious Merciful did not mind breaking the anti-kickback laws, so I would not rule out the possibility that Merciful would go outside the law in other ways to fight me. I took into consideration all of that, but I still wanted to file the lawsuit because I couldn't survive under the present circumstances. If I was going down anyway, I might as well file the lawsuit and go down fighting.

But Walter *would not file it*. Instead, he took up my time with lawyerly discussions, which continued to be eloquent and quite profound, but never seemed to get us to a definite decision about what to do next.

And Walter continued his hours and hours of interminable discussions with Ann Paget. Walter was quite discreet and secretive about the substance of these conversations, except to say that they were "productive" or "helpful." Well, they were productive of billable time for Walter, which I'm sure was helpful to his firm. But the discussions weren't doing anything for me, and as we came to the end of June, there was no end of the nightmare in sight.

CHAPTER 25

June 2017

Enough about the facts. What was going on with *me*?

I was a mess.

Until Merciful came after me, I believed that if I studied hard and worked hard, obeyed the rules, and tried to be a good person, good things would happen to me; I thought that loyalty and integrity were virtues and would be rewarded. It was like I had a pact, not with the devil, but with the universe, that if I obeyed the rules and did not do bad things, then bad things would not happen to me. That's not *too crazy*, is it?

But these beliefs were blown away like mobile homes in a tornado when this awful thing happened to me, something that to my knowledge had never occurred to any other business or person. I was facing financial ruin, but that was not unusual; plenty of businesses and individuals face financial ruin – happens all the time – businesses succeed and fail, that's capitalism. But other companies and persons have the option of walking away from debts or declaring bankruptcy. My dilemma, which seemed unique, was that I couldn't walk away or declare bankruptcy because of patient care issues – I was the custodian of specimens from patients that were needed for present and future care.

So even that worst-case scenario for other companies – going bankrupt and losing everything – was not an option for me. I couldn't stay in business with a liability of $750,000.00, and I couldn't declare bankruptcy or walk away. No one wanted to buy the company. There were no options for me. I couldn't fully comprehend what was happening to me.

I just knew that it was terrible. I simply could not have anticipated what was happening to me. Franz Kafka describes such an experience in his book *The Trial*. But *The Trial* was written as fiction, probably as a metaphor for life. In real life I had never heard of something like this happening to anyone. Such a thing seemed impossible to me, but it was happening, and there seemed to be no way to stop it.

CHAPTER 26

July 2017

July 1

It was a Saturday night, and I couldn't sleep. I kept worrying about my company and what was going to happen to me. If I kept working under the present circumstances, I would go broke. If I closed the business and walked away, the authorities would come after me for jeopardizing patient care. No one was willing to help my company file for bankruptcy. No one wanted to buy it. How did I get myself into this mess? I was reminded of the scene in the movie *The Sand Pebbles* when the Steve McQueen character, Jake Holman, is cornered and about to be killed by enemy forces, and he says, "I was home. What happened? What the hell happened?"

Well, I was "Jack" instead of "Jake," but I had similar feelings. "I had a company," I thought. "What happened? What the hell happened?"

Since I couldn't sleep, I got out of bed and tried not to wake my wife, Sarah, as I picked up my iPhone from the top of the dresser. I went next door to my study, sat at my desk, and sent an e-mail to Walter that went like this:

Dear Walter Sneed,

I am having trouble sleeping tonight, which is happening a lot. So if I can't sleep, I might as well write. Your metaphor that I'm a bull in the china shop is apt, but it's not like I went into the china shop of my own free will; it's like I was captured and released there, with no way out.

On the one hand, there seems to be little chance of settling the case. Merciful is more interested in getting me into "compliance" (which to them means not billing Merciful for pathology lab costs) than they are on reaching an agreement. In addition, you are "uncomfortable" with any settlement that allows Merciful to keep any of the money they have already taken from me, because that could be construed as giving away my services for various benefits, in other words, a kickback, which would violate Stark law. Interestingly, Merciful seems to have no problem whatsoever doing what you regard as a violation of Stark law. In fact, they do not seem to be bothered in the least by any of the laws they are breaking. So, to summarize, if I bill Merciful for the lab costs, Merciful says I am not in compliance with their policies. If I don't bill Merciful, you say I am not in compliance with federal law.

I don't see any way this gets settled without a lawsuit.

Yet you refuse to file a lawsuit. Or file an injunction. Or do anything else. You tell me that we can't do such things because Merciful can fight back by kicking me off the provider lists for their insurance plans and opposing the lawsuit with an army of attorneys and other resources and "using ERISA law to fight me" (whatever that means). At any rate, according to you "Merciful holds all the cards." So you refuse to file your well-reasoned, well-written lawsuit and injunction, which I have signed and notarized. It just sits there.

We did file a Reconsideration Appeal. Unfortunately, it was ineffective. Merciful denied the appeal after waiting to respond until the last possible minute of the last possible day. The denial was unconvincing. You know and I know and I am sure Merciful knows that what Merciful is doing is indefensible and would not withstand scrutiny.

So when are we going to fight? I know you perceive me to be impulsive and impatient, and I know the denial of our appeal only happened a few days ago. But recoupment has been going on for at least a month and is continuing, even though Merciful says otherwise. The executives at Merciful must be laughing their heads off about all the free work they are getting from me. The joke's on Jack.

Sela and I have sent you everything you have asked for, which is everything under the sun. I have signed affidavits, notarized documents, and followed through on every request you have made. To get you the information you need, I have either phoned or met with everyone you have asked me to contact. After all this...nothing.

You craft these eloquent lawyerly documents – lawsuits and injunctions, draft after draft, which I read carefully, but then nothing happens except for "good conversations" with Ann Paget, who tells you that the recoupments that are happening are not happening, or that they "can't stop them."

There is no business plan whatsoever that works if Merciful does not pay for the services that I am providing their patients. You are probably right that if we file a lawsuit, Merciful "has all the cards" and will bankrupt me and crush my company like a bug and not think twice about it. What I can't seem to get across to you, though, is that even if we don't file the lawsuit, Merciful will bankrupt me, crush me like a bug, and not think twice about it. The probable result is the same either way.

I prefer to go down fighting. File the darn lawsuit and injunction. I don't see how I can make my wishes any clearer. Thanks.

Jack

I pressed send about midnight on that Saturday night.

CHAPTER 27

July 2017

Walter phoned me first thing Monday morning. He didn't want to file the lawsuit and injunction. He said, "If you just stick with me, Jack, I think my approach has a good chance of success."

"What's your approach?"

"I think I am getting through to Ann Paget and Merciful that they have a real compliance issue on their hands – that they are breaking the law. They can't use their market power to get things from you for free, a kickback if you will – it's illegal. I sense that Ann Paget is working behind the scenes to get Merciful executives to understand this."

"That's all fine and good, but something had better happen soon, or any remedy will happen too late to help me. I seem to have trouble getting this concept across to you."

"Just don't do anything rash, like declaring bankruptcy or selling the company, without talking to me first."

"Okay."

CHAPTER 28

July 2017

Walter must have been hearing encouraging things from Ann Paget that he didn't share with me. But I didn't like this reticence and secretiveness. His attitude of "trust me I know what I am doing" and "your lawyer knows best" was driving me nuts.

I was losing faith in Walter. To me it was like an incompetent doctor had a soothing bedside manner while the patient died from his malpractice – holding the hands of a dying patient and mouthing platitudes while the patient died due to the doctor's ineptitude. Listening to Walter's platitudes, I felt like a dying patient.

And no one cared, not Merciful, not Excel Pinnacle, not my fellow physicians, no one. I had trouble facing that obvious fact. I thought that what I was doing, pathology, was important. Turns out, it wasn't. No one cared. It hurt.

I don't think I am unique in experiencing that hurt, that disappointment. Life is filled with letdowns. Teachers have students who are unappreciative to say the least. So many artists paint pictures that are ignored. Most writers toil in obscurity and cannot even earn enough from their writing to make a decent income. So an unappreciated pathologist? What's the big deal?

Of course it's not a big deal. Most of us live lives that are of negligible significance. We go through life doing our best, working so hard knowing that what we do has infinitesimal effects. So why go on?

Because it's heroic. To continue anyway, to do the best you can. One's purpose has to come from within, to take pride in one's work, one's art. If you are looking outside for validation, it ain't gonna happen.

CHAPTER 29

July 2017

Since I no longer had any trust in Walter, I turned to someone I did trust – Raymond Scott, the attorney that Pathology Services had on retainer, who had provided excellent legal advice to me for decades. I told him my concerns, that nothing seemed to be happening, and that if things continued on their present course, I would be out of business sooner rather than later. And that Walter didn't seem to grasp this concept.

I asked Raymond if we could do a conference call – Walter, Raymond, and me – so that Raymond could give me an assessment of whether Walter was providing acceptable legal service or not.

The call happened a few days later. Walter started out by summarizing what had happened so far. I then brought up the idea of selling the company.

"How are you going to keep the pathologists you have if you sell?" asked Walter.

I said, "I'll have to negotiate new contracts with the pathologists to induce them to stay. This business isn't worth much without pathologists."

"Okay," said Walter.

Then I learned a lot of stuff I wish Walter had been telling me all along.

Concerning my fight with Merciful, Walter said he was not going to wait for arbitration. In his opinion, Merciful would just use this as a delaying tactic – not agreeing on the makeup of the arbitration panel, delaying the meetings, and so forth. Walter wanted to go straight to the lawsuit.

I said I was fine with that. In fact, why hadn't he filed it yet?

Walter said that he was using it as a threat, to try to get Merciful to settle.

Raymond didn't say much, just listened. But when we wrapped up, Raymond said, "Jack, stay on the line after Walter hangs up."

After Walter dropped off, Raymond said, "I think you are in good hands. Sometimes I do what Walter is doing, use the threat of a lawsuit to induce the other side to settle. I think it has a good chance of success."

That sounded good to me. But it had to happen soon. I was running out of time.

CHAPTER 30

July 2017

I didn't think much was going to happen for the next week or two, so I went on vacation. Sarah and I had a previously scheduled two-week trip to a resort on Little Cayman Island. Importantly, the trip was already paid for, back before Merciful attacked me. Little Cayman is a small Caribbean Island with a population of about 150 people. There's nothing to do there but scuba dive (which I love to do) and fish (which I don't do). A perfect getaway.

I told Walter I was going away for a couple of weeks and where I was going. I told him that Little Cayman was remote with little infrastructure, and I asked him not to bother me unless something really significant happened. My fight with Merciful had consumed me for three months, and I needed a break, or I was going to have a nervous breakdown, if I wasn't in the midst of one already. I was obsessed by this fight. Walter agreed that nothing much was going to happen over the next few weeks, and to have a good time.

I did.

Each morning Sarah and I went scuba diving. In the afternoon I went scuba diving again or took a nap or read a book or some combination of the three. At five o'clock Sarah and I picked up a rum punch at the bar. Then we walked to the dock and watched the sunset until it was time for dinner. After dinner it was bedtime.

Rinse and repeat.

After about a week of this, I felt pretty good. I didn't hear anything about Merciful, Excel Pinnacle, the audit, or our proposed lawsuit.

CHAPTER 31

July 2017

This matter with Merciful started in April and continued through May, June, and well into July with no interruption. After months of strife, I saw no hope of a good outcome. I couldn't surrender and survive, and I saw no hints of any compromise in Merciful's position. It seemed as if my nightmare would never end.

And then it did.

CHAPTER 32

July 2017

I was still on vacation late in the afternoon of July 17, a Monday, when Walter sent me this e-mail:

"Jack,

I'm going to bother you, but I think you will forgive me. Below I'm including a copy of my Memo of Record of my conversation with Ann Paget. I'm pretty sure you will consider it good news. Let me know if you got this. Hope you are having a good trip. I hope to have one when we get this resolved! Walter"

The Memo of Record went like this:

Memo of Record

Ann Paget telephoned me on the afternoon of July 17, 2017, to discuss a proposal to resolve the case. I believe it will be well received by you.

The proposal is that any further efforts to take back the $750,000.00 Merciful says you owe would stop. You keep the money. Further, all the charges you submit will be paid until September 2017. There will be no more money takebacks or claim denials.

Between now and September 2017, Merciful will issue documentation that will go out to all physician providers, which states that effective October 1, 2017, pathology lab costs will be paid only to the hospital, not to you or any other independent pathology lab, and Merciful will amend the Provider Administration Manual to say exactly that.

I questioned whether the funds that had already been taken would be returned to you. Ann Paget said that at this point she had not been authorized to make that offer, but reading between the lines, it sounded to me as if that issue had not been discussed. She said that is something that could be raised in a counteroffer and that consideration may be given whether or not it is worth litigating over an amount she believes to be $25,000.00. (Our figures today showed $45,517.00, but there is a question as to whether some of that relates to other issues, which I am still trying to find out about.) She was going to request updated amounts from Merciful. It certainly sounded as if those funds would be refunded to you if we asked for Merciful to do so. I asked her to go ahead and address that with Merciful, because retaining those funds would not be right. **I did not, however, reject her proposal as it presently stands.**

I questioned what the result would be that if come October 1, 2017, the hospital still contends that it has not been paid the pathology lab costs expense, and thus would not pass on the money to Dr. Spenser's Pathology Services Laboratory. She felt that the additional documentation and the changes to the Merciful Provider Manual would bring the issue to a head.

Ann Paget said that their plan was to still take the position that the bundled payments to the hospital include the pathology lab costs. I responded that this created logistical problems, but what they do in the future is not a concern of this litigation.

Of note, Ms. Paget began this whole discussion by saying that Merciful's primary concern is prospective compliance.

    Walter

I phoned Walter immediately after I read his e-mail. I said, "I want to accept their offer as is."

Walter was in essential agreement with this. He said, "Here's the deal: This offer on the table from Merciful is a contract. Merciful has made it, and it is binding. They cannot retract it. We can accept it or reject it. If we agree to it, it is binding, it is a contract, and we are done except for dotting the i's and crossing the t's. If we make a counteroffer, then their offer is off the table, and we start from scratch."

I said, "I don't want to outsmart myself. One time many years ago, there was a house that we liked that we wanted to buy, but another party also liked the house a lot and had already put in a bid on it, which had been accepted by the seller, with some very trivial changes. However, instead of accepting these quite fair conditions, the other party who had gotten there first made counteroffers with contingencies, trying to out negotiate the seller and get a really sweet deal on the house. But we knew it was a sellers' market, so we made a simple straightforward offer agreeing to the seller's conditions, and we ended up with a great house. The other party negotiated themselves right out of a good deal; they were furious and fired their real estate agent.

I think something similar could happen here. If I ask for the money already collected by Merciful, I'm afraid they will regard this as greedy and think to themselves: "Hey, we made Spenser a good offer, and now he comes back with this? Tell me again why we are settling this case? Let's forget the whole settlement thing and litigate this. Spenser wants to fight? Bring it on."

I finished my soliloquy and said, "Accept Merciful's offer as is."

Walter said, "As you know, I have issues with letting the previously taken money go, from a compliance standpoint, but I think your comments have merit. You want to get this matter behind you."

"Look, Walter, from the very start of this nightmare, all I have wanted is to be treated like every other pathologist in the state. I can live with whatever happens on October 1. Pathology Services is a very efficient operation, and we work hard. We can match or exceed whatever terms other groups want to try to negotiate with Excel Pinnacle and Merciful after the Provider Manual update and any other policies that apply to everyone."

"Okay."

I had other reasons not to try to get back the money Merciful had already taken from me, whether it was $25,000.00 or $45,517.00:

1. One obvious reason right off the bat is that Merciful and I differed on the amounts at stake – was it $25,000.00 or $45,517.00? Trying to resolve this issue would be an accounting nightmare. Sorting out the proper amount of money to be returned to Pathology Services would take time and effort from me, Sela, Merciful's business office,

Ann Paget, and last but not least, Walter, who would be charging me $350.00 an hour.

2. And then even if we agreed on a figure, the logistics to get this money from Merciful would be formidable. I knew this from experience in the past when Merciful underpaid me and owed my company money. What Merciful definitely *would not do* is simply write Pathology Services a check for the amount they owed. No, no, no. That would be too simple, and nothing was simple when it came to getting paid by insurance companies. What would happen is that we would have to resubmit each charge for each patient, and Merciful would have to install a reprogrammed computer "patch" that would include these payments in future reimbursements. Of course, like any computer programming, that patch might or might not work, which would mean more computer programming and resubmitting charges yet again, which would mean extensive talks with computer programmers and reimbursement specialists at Merciful to try to get my money. The amount of money at stake just wasn't worth the hassle.

3. I didn't want to get greedy. My company could survive a hit of $25,000.00 or $45,517.00. It could not survive a hit of $767,655.28 – the amount the "audit" said I owed.

4. Merciful, in my opinion, was not willing to come out of this incident with nothing, not even enough to pay for the costs of this so-called "audit." That would be a money loser, and if I knew one thing about Merciful, they hated to lose money. At least the money already recouped would help pay Merciful's costs for this unfortunate matter and help Merciful save face. I just couldn't believe Merciful would consent to end this matter with absolutely nothing to show for it.

A few days later, when I was still on vacation, I got an e-mail with an attachment documenting the official settlement offer from Merciful. It was straightforward, short, and simple:

1. Merciful ceases all efforts to take back the money Merciful contends is outstanding related to the audits.

2. Merciful agrees that it will not conduct further audits or issue denials for the pathology lab cost charges rendered for claims submitted prior to October 1, 2017.

I sent a reply to Walter: "Okay to settle. Thanks."

Walter phoned me a few minutes later, and I repeated my position that we accept the settlement offer from Merciful as proposed, with no counteroffer.

Walter continued to protect his rear end. A couple of hours later I received this e-mail:

"Jack, I'm attaching a letter that summarizes our important conversation this afternoon, and another attachment with a draft of a letter I intend to send to Ann Paget in the morning. Glad you are pleased with this resolution. Hope the rest of your vacation is enjoyable."

The first attachment said this:

"I received your e-mail confirming your instructions to accept the Merciful offer in its present form. We discussed that the proposal does not require that Merciful reimburse the amounts that had been previously recouped, but Merciful says that only $25,000.00 relates to the lab costs issue. I suggested to Ann Paget that the previously recouped money should be refunded. She did not rule out that possibility, but she did not have authority to offer that, and said that it may be something we want to request in a counteroffer. You and I discussed that a counteroffer is in effect a rejection of their offer, whereas acceptance of their offer is a contract. I proposed at least simply asking Ann Paget about refunding the recouped payments, but you instructed me not to do that, and simply accept the proposal as is."

The second attachment, the proposed letter to Ann Paget, was short and sweet:

"Jack Spenser, M.D., on behalf of Pathology Services, PC, has instructed me to accept these terms."

I sent this e-mail:

"Walter, your letter accurately summarizes our important conversation today. The draft of the letter to Ann Paget is also satisfactory. I am most pleased with this resolution. 'Thanks' hardly does justice to your efforts on behalf of Pathology Services, PC. Jack"

VICTORY!! Stripped of all the jargon, I got 95% of what I wanted. The settlement was essentially a big NEVER MIND from Merciful. My war with Merciful was over.

CHAPTER 33

July 2017

I would like to end the story here, and what a great story it is!

First, there was the wrongdoing, the tort, the crime: a large company (Merciful) attacked a small company (Pathology Services) and tried to squash it for the sake of greed.

Second, there were the sympathetic victims, heroes if you will, working men and women – the ER docs, the hospitalists, the employees of Pathology Services, and your humble narrator, a pathologist, all of whom just wanted to be left alone to take care of patients.

Third, there were the evildoers, the largest health insurance company in the state and the largest hospital corporation in the country – two unsympathetic antagonists/opponents. Virtually everyone has some horror story to tell about his or her interactions with health insurers and hospitals.

Fourth, if I end it here, at least once, the side that had minimal resources (me) went against a foe with great resources (the insurance company) and won in spite of overwhelming odds against such an outcome – a very compelling narrative. The insurance company caved in. Merciful did not collect the three-quarters of a million dollars they wrongfully said I had to pay, and Merciful agreed to pay my pathology lab costs going forward, at least for a while.

Any reader has to love this story so far, in which the underdog won. A filmmaker could take my story and make a great movie out of it. Nothing delights a moviegoer more than a tale of triumph over injustice. A story with this arc is a winner. That's why over half the films made today are a variation of this theme: the underdog wins in spite of overwhelming odds against an evil foe with superior resources. It's escape fiction. So I should end this book right here.

Unfortunately, I can't. It would be a fairy tale. In real life this kind of outcome doesn't happen. Or at least it doesn't happen very often.

Alas, this is not one of those stories where the good guys win. This is real life.

CHAPTER 34

September 2017–December 2018

Initially, everything looked hopeful. After all the paperwork was completed, Merciful resumed paying all my charges. Pathology Services was profitable again, very profitable.

Merciful continued to pay Pathology Services for my pathology lab costs through September of 2017, just as they agreed to. Then they did something extra; they paid all my charges through the rest of 2017. Then Merciful did even more yet and paid all my charges through January, February, and March of 2018, long after Merciful had planned to stop paying for such services. Finally, Merciful even agreed to pay all my charges to the end of 2018. Those were halcyon days for Pathology Services.

It was time to sell my company.

Which I did in June of 2018. The buyer was Rural Pathology Group, which was about the same size company as mine and based in a town about sixty miles away. The owners were two pathologists, Jeff Franklin and Sid McElroy, who were in their thirties. Buying Pathology Services gave them a footprint near Midwest City. As part of the purchase agreement, I agreed to stay involved in the day-to-day operations of Pathology Services for two years. Unfortunately that meant I would get to see the downfall of Pathology Services firsthand.

For the first two months after the sale, things were great. Then on August 20, 2018, Merciful sent an amendment to the contract between Pathology Services and Merciful affirming that Merciful regarded the bundled payments to Excel Pinnacle Hospital as including the payment to Pathology Services for pathology lab costs, and that the lack of any response within thirty days constituted acceptance of that provision. The new contract went into effect on December 31, 2018. On that date reimbursements for pathology lab costs to Pathology Services would end, and there wasn't a darn thing Pathology Services could do about it. We couldn't make Merciful pay for the pathology lab costs any more than a beneficiary could demand Merciful pay for fish oil, one-a-day vitamins, massages, heart/lung transplants, or anything else not in the contract. And dropping our contract with Merciful was not an option, because Merciful-insured patients would still come to Excel Pinnacle Hospital, and our contract with the hospital said we had to provide pathology services to those patients whether we got paid or not.

The only solution was to request payment from Excel Pinnacle Hospital to Pathology Services for pathology lab costs incurred by Merciful-insured patients. I thought this was a reasonable request. After all, Merciful contended that Excel Pinnacle Hospital was getting reimbursed for such costs from Merciful; it seemed fair that the hospital would pass on those payments to Pathology Services. There was even a precedent for such a policy: Excel Pinnacle Hospital was already passing on to Pathology Services the payments for pathology lab costs that it was getting from Medicare. I thought it would be simple enough to apply this policy to Merciful-insured patients.

I thought wrong. Excel Pinnacle Hospital kept all the money they received from Merciful and did not pass on any of it to Pathology Services. They kept the money and expected us to eat the costs, i.e., provide the service for free.

This is the way that sordid chapter unfolded: Since I had a long history with Excel Pinnacle Hospital, the new owners of the company asked me to make the request to the Excel Pinnacle executives that they pass on to Pathology Services the money that Merciful contended they were paying Excel Pinnacle Hospital for services Pathology Services was providing. I scheduled a meeting with the management of Excel Pinnacle to make this request.

Bart Magnum, the CEO of the hospital, was too busy to see me. David Turner, the COO, did meet with me and Sela. We met in the boardroom of the hospital.

David Turner, speaking for the hospital administration, refused to pay Pathology Services anything to cover the costs of operating the pathology lab. He said, "Your contract with Excel Pinnacle Hospital clearly states that Pathology Services is responsible for all anatomic pathology services, and that includes the costs of running your laboratory."

I said, "Merciful says the payments to you for their patients include the costs of running our laboratory, and that you are supposed to pass those funds on to us."

David said, "We don't care what Merciful says. Oh, and if you at Pathology Services don't like the contract you have with us, well, we talked to Federated Pathologists yesterday, and they can be here tomorrow providing pathology services to us with the same contract you don't want to accept, including not getting paid anything whatsoever from us."

"Why are you doing this to us?" I asked. "You know it's wrong." I really wanted to know.

"Because we are Excel Corp, and we are big, and we can."

He really said that.

This is a story of corruption and lawlessness. What Merciful and Excel did to me was illegal.

But no one cared. Walter informed the State Commissioner of Insurance about what was going on, that Merciful and Excel were demanding free services from us, which is against various state and federal laws against kickbacks. The State Commissioner of Insurance took a Pontius Pilate approach. In his written reply he said, "We don't get involved in contract negotiations."

CHAPTER 35

January 2019–August 2019

Well, that was the end of Pathology Services, PC. I'm sure I've made it painfully clear to my very patient readers that Pathology Services could not survive without reimbursement for the pathology lab costs provided to Merciful-insured patients. And it didn't.

Unfortunately, the death of Pathology Services, PC, was slow and painful. Dr. Franklin and Dr. McElroy, the new owners of Pathology Services, went down fighting. With the resultant decrease in revenues from Merciful, they downsized the company; they terminated almost everyone employed by Pathology Services, including all the laboratory workers and all the typists/transcriptionists. The three pathologists employed by Pathology Services didn't like the changes and left – one retired, one took a job at a hospital in Midwest City, and the third moved to Southern California. Dr. Franklin and Dr. McElroy closed the Pathology Services laboratory and moved the instruments, computers, paraffin blocks, tissue specimens, microscopic slides, and equipment to their Rural Pathology laboratory facility. Then the tasks that Pathology Services were doing for Excel Pinnacle Hospital were transferred to their existing Rural Pathology Group lab facility, fifty miles from Pathfinder, with all the logistical challenges that entailed. Plus, there was no increase in staff to replace the workers terminated at Pathology Services – no more laboratory workers and no more typists/transcriptionists – not one more worker to handle the increased workload. The result was that the same number of employees at Rural Pathology were doing twice as much work – the work they were already doing for Rural Pathology plus all the additional work that Pathology Services needed done.

These changes looked great on the spreadsheets and kept the company profitable, but didn't work very well for taking care of patients. Not surprisingly, the pathology service at Excel Pinnacle Hospital went down in quality. For example, surgical pathology reports for tissue specimens were delayed. Prior to the staff cutbacks, Pathology Services had a one-day turnaround time to report the results of our tissue specimen examinations. For example, if a small tissue sample (biopsy) of tissue – e.g., breast, prostate gland, skin, brain, or other organ – was collected on a Monday, almost always a pathology report by our department was available on Tuesday. Then the patient's physician could reassure the patient if the lesion was benign, or begin treatment for an inflammatory condition, or make plans for further follow-up and treatment if the lesion was malignant. In summary, those decisions could be made by the patient and the patient's physician the next day after the tissue was removed, because that's when our report was ready. For larger tissue specimens like colon resections, breast lumpectomies, removal of lung lobes, or other complicated specimens, our turnaround time might not be one day, but even reports for these complex specimens were ready in a couple of days.

Of course, to achieve those quick turnaround times, it took a lot of effort from the pathologists (to dissect the tissue and examine the microscopic slides of that tissue), laboratory workers (to process the tissue samples overnight and prepare the microscopic slides the next morning), and typists (to produce the report). To get all this done in twenty-four hours was a daily challenge, which couldn't be met after the dramatic cutbacks in the number of Pathology Services' employees. Work piled up and backed up, and turnaround times went from twenty-four hours to several days or even weeks. These delays caused wailing and gnashing of teeth from the surgeons, oncologists, and other doctors taking care of the patients. The following episode was typical:

It happened when I attended the monthly meeting of hospital Executive Committee. After the meeting, Dr. Andy Spickard (a surgeon who was also the chief of the medical staff) and Dr. Jane Haverford (an oncologist) walked over to where I was sitting. Andy said, "We have to talk." Jane nodded her head in agreement.

I said, "Okay."

Andy asked, "Has there been some change in the pathology department? Did you sell the company?"

"Yes."

After the meeting, I was still sitting down. Andy and Jane towered over me and then delivered a litany of complaints, emphasizing the delay in getting reports and the problems that caused.

Andy said, "Patients come into my office for follow-up visits after their surgery, and I can't tell them anything because I don't have the pathology results back. I can't tell them if what I took out was benign or malignant, whether I got the entire tumor out and the surgical margins are clear, or whether I have to go back in and reoperate...I can't tell them anything."

Jane chimed in and said, "Breast cancer patients come into my office, and I don't know whether the next step is radiation therapy, chemotherapy, or both, or nothing further...I just don't know because I have no pathology reports. I don't know the type of breast cancer or the results of special studies like hormone receptor status, or whether the cancer has spread to the lymph nodes – I don't know anything! So the patient visits to my office are useless, a waste of time. It's so bad that my nurses have to check the patients' charts each day and look to see of the pathology reports are there, and if they are not available, my nurse has to phone the patients to reschedule the appointments. What a nuisance!"

After listening to these and similar complaints, I stood up. I said, "You need to talk to Jeff Franklin, the president of the group. He needs to hear this."

Both shook their heads. Neither one of them wanted to do that. After the Executive Committee meeting, they were already behind on the day, and they wanted to get to work taking care of patients. There were operations to do, and patients to check on.

"Jeff Franklin needs to hear this," I repeated.

So Jeff Franklin did indeed hear the complaints. Reluctantly, Dr. Spickard and Dr. Haverford walked with me to Jeff's office in the hospital lab. As we entered his office, he was looking through his microscope. Jeff pushed his chair away from the microscope and his desk and greeted us.

I sat down in one of the chairs in the office and started the discussion by nodding to Dr. Spickard and Dr. Haverford. "You know Andy Spickard and Jane Haverford," I said. They remained standing.

"Of course," said Jeff.

Andy and Jane remained standing as they told Jeff their complaints, the same ones I had heard earlier. Jeff listened, occasionally nodding up and down as Andy and Jane were speaking. Jeff occasionally interjected comments like "I understand" or "I agree" or "That's unacceptable." When Andy and Jane were finished with their diatribe, Jeff said, "We have to do better."

"You sure do," said Andy.

Jane said, "We have not gone to the hospital administration about these issues — yet — because we want to give you a chance to correct things. We'll give you a couple of weeks, and if things are not better, we will go to Bart Magnum and talk to him about these problems."

I saw no chance that things would get better. Everyone was already working as hard as they could. We needed more laboratory workers and transcriptionists to meet the demands of our clinicians and patients. Without lab costs reimbursement money from Merciful or Excel Pinnacle or somebody, there were no funds to pay the employees we needed.

And here is the saddest part of the story: Even if funds were available, it was too late to re-establish Pathology Services. The terminated lab workers and transcriptionists with decades of experience and training were gone, having moved on to other things, other jobs, and other interests. Even if there were funds available to rehire them, they would not come back to Pathology Services, a company that had fired them. Any replacements we could find might be talented and intelligent, but they would not have the decades of experience of those who were let go, and would not know the Pathology Services culture that had been around for fifty years. Pathology Services was gone and not coming back, ever.

CHAPTER 36

September 2019

Sure enough, the service we provided to the Excel Pinnacle Hospital and its doctors did not improve, and the complaints about Pathology Services, PC, grew louder and more frequent. These complaints reached the ears of Bart Magnum and other executives of the hospital. Bart Magnum met several times with Jeff Franklin and Sid McElroy and demanded improvements in service. "You have to do something to correct this," said Bart Magnum.

Didn't happen.

We lost the Excel Pinnacle Hospital pathology contract in September 2019. Thus ended the tenure of Pathology Services, which had provided pathology services to Excel Pinnacle Hospital for almost fifty years, starting when the hospital was built. We were the only pathology group the hospital had ever had.

I was the first pathologist in our group to hear the news. It happened when I attended the routine monthly Executive Committee meeting in September, something I had been doing for decades. Bart Magnum, as CEO of Excel Pinnacle Hospital, always ended the meeting with his "Administrator's Report." At the end of his report, he made the announcement that there would be a change in pathology vendors – Pathology Services was terminated, and Federated Pathology Inc. would take our place. In a perfunctory manner Bart thanked me for my years of service to the hospital. End of meeting.

But before that happened, I made a brief impromptu statement, having had no notice that this announcement was going to be made. I simply thanked everyone there for the opportunity to provide pathology services to their patients for all these years up till the present. I hope I projected a feeling of gratitude, not bitterness.

This was hard to do. A few days later I found out from a friend of mine who worked at Federated Laboratories that Excel Pinnacle Hospital was going to pay Federated for the pathology lab costs of Merciful-insured patients. I found it incredibly sad that Excel Pinnacle immediately did for Federated what they absolutely refused to do for us.

CHAPTER 37

September 2019 to present

Shortly after all this went down, it was time for my yearly checkup with Dr. Bob Newcombe. My health was good, so the exam didn't take long. In the time left over, we talked about what had happened to me and Pathology Services. Dr. Newcombe said these wise words to me:

"What I am about to say has nothing to do with your health. Pretend I'm your 'uncle Bob' talking. I want your attitude about what happened to be one of *gratitude* for a long, productive, and rewarding career. I don't want you to become one of those old bitter doctors who get forced out, and then spend the rest of their lives missing medicine and complaining to God and anyone else who will listen about the ingratitude of patients, hospitals, Medicare, and the insurance companies – and how they were so mistreated. They can't move on. That's not a good way to spend time in God's waiting room. I don't want that to happen to you."

I thought that this was great advice, from a true physician who was not only taking care of my body, but also my mind and spirit. So I tried to take the high road and just be grateful for a pathology career at Excel Pinnacle that lasted over forty years. It was a great run, but it was over. I said nothing derogatory about the hospital. Similarly I did not disparage Federated Laboratories, continuing my policy of not badmouthing the competition. Plus, I had friends who worked there.

And in fairness to Federated and Excel Pinnacle, they both made a real effort to keep me on as a staff pathologist at Excel Pinnacle Hospital, and as a physician/pathologist employee of Federated

Laboratories. This wasn't done out of kindness. It apparently dawned on Bart Magnum, after he fired us, that there was no guarantee that Federated would do a better job than Pathology Services – that what was going to happen was a bunch of new pathologists would show up to work at the hospital, and who knew whether they would fit in or not. Similarly, Federated knew that there was a nationwide shortage of pathologists, and not just any pathologist could step in and do the pathology job Excel Pinnacle wanted done. Excel Pinnacle was known to be a very demanding hospital, bordering on the unreasonable. So a couple of weeks after Pathology Services was summarily terminated, Bart Magnum told me that he very much wanted me to stay on, and in fact he *needed* me to stay on. To that end, Federated made me an offer to work for them – a very generous offer that I was tempted to accept.

However, I declined. I turned down the position not out of any revenge or an "up yours" reaction. The reason I passed on the offer to stay on is that I did not think I could do the job that Excel Pinnacle and Federated wanted me to do. My experience has been that if you change one thing, you change everything. I was used to being an *owner* of Pathology Services, a company with four pathologists and twenty employees. If I stayed on at Excel Pinnacle, I would be an *employee* of Federated, which had over a hundred pathologists and thousands of employees. When I was an owner, I had a lot of clout and a lot of control over working conditions and quality. As an employee, I would have very little clout and very little control over working conditions and the quality of what happened around me. I thought it likely that Federated and I would be a bad fit. My considered opinion was that if I stayed on, it would be a lose-lose-lose outcome for the hospital, Federated, and me.

Sela and I were kept on by Rural Pathology Group to help out with the remainder of their operations after Excel Pinnacle no longer wanted our services. I went to work for them, mainly doing the pathology at a northern suburban hospital in Midwest City, which was aptly named Northern Suburban Hospital. It was about the same size as Excel Pinnacle Hospital. After I had been there a while, Northern Suburban Hospital was acquired by Midwest Medical

Center, a large academic medical institution, the place where I went to medical school and trained to be a pathologist about half a century earlier. Since that time Midwest Medical Center had grown by expanding its campus and by buying additional hospitals throughout the Midwest, indeed, throughout the country. Midwest Medical Center had grown to the extent that it was bigger than Merciful and almost the size of Excel Corp. After the purchase, Midwest Medical Center changed the name of the hospital from "Northern Suburban Hospital" to "Midwest Medical Center at Northern Suburban Midwest City." I thought that this was a rather cumbersome name, but I'm just a humble pathologist, not a high-powered, highly paid healthcare executive responsible for leading the thousands of people employed by Midwest Medical Center.

Rural Pathology Group kept the pathology contract, and I kept working as a pathologist at Midwest Medical Center at Northern Suburban Midwest City. I became one of the thousands of physicians employed by Midwest Medical Center, even though I still worked for Rural Pathology Group. I know all of this sounds complicated, but let me make it very simple: I went corporate.

CHAPTER 38

It's time to wrap up the story of Pathology Services, PC. On the surface, this is a story about change. And change is good, right? I had my run, helped a lot of patients, got paid well, sold my company, and let the next generation take over. That's life.

In some ways life is like a relay race where you have your turn on the track, run as fast as you can, and then give the baton to the next runner, or in this case, the next pathology group. A cursory summary is that this is the story of a bigger company (Federated Laboratories) beating out a smaller company (Pathology Services) for the pathology business at Excel Pinnacle Hospital. That's the way capitalism is supposed to work, right? It's the American way, competition; the best company wins. What's wrong with that?

Here's what's wrong: The contest is rigged. When we at Pathology Services competed in a fair contest against Federated, or any other lab company, big or small — we whipped their butts. For fifty years we kept the Excel Pinnacle contract because we had well-trained hardworking pathologists and a staff of twenty employees who reliably provided a high-quality pathology service. We were never sued for malpractice. Our turnaround time was almost always twenty-four hours — i.e., patients and their doctors almost always had the pathology reports of their specimens available the next day. Our service was unsurpassed.

Pathology Services did not lose the pathology contract at Excel Pinnacle because another company came along with better services or better prices. We lost the contract because companies with billions of dollars in revenues, Merciful and Excel, didn't obey the rules and pay us for the pathology lab work we did, which destroyed our company. And a third company, Federated, with several hundred million dollars in revenues, came in and picked up the pieces.

CHAPTER 39

So one more small company, Pathology Services, PC, disappeared without a trace. The event was so insignificant that it was not heralded anywhere – no newspaper notices, no TV coverage, no announcements on the radio, and nothing on the internet. There was a similar lack of fanfare when I left the medical staff of Excel Pinnacle Hospital after forty-one years – no retirement dinner, no reception with punch and cookies, and no watch or any other parting gift. I didn't even get a cake.

CHAPTER 40

Present day

After some time for reflection, I decided to heed the requests of my colleagues and tell the tale of what happened to me and my fellow physicians. This is my fourth book. I have modest expectations for it. That's okay. I'm not sure I want it to "hit." If it becomes a best seller, then Merciful and Excel might come after me. They almost destroyed me the first time around. This time they may finish the job.

But I had to write this book. Look, we have big problems in this country, and big problems in healthcare. I hope this little book gives some understanding of the changes that are happening in medicine, which in some ways are deleterious. This tale is obviously told from my perspective, which may or may not be fair. Other players in the healthcare arena – insurance companies and hospital corporations – are entitled to their viewpoints as well; hopefully they will tell their stories and enter the discourse. I would love to read any literature they put out.

In the meantime, I want this book to be a document of a time and place in medicine, one physician's story, and a resource so that my readers in the present and future will know what happened. Hopefully this little story tells a big story. I cannot tell THE BIG STORY of the HEALTHCARE CRISIS IN AMERICA – who the villains are, and who the heroes are, and exactly what happened. I don't have the time, energy, or investigative skills to write a long nonfiction book about what happened to our great American healthcare system, and how to fix it. I'm not a journalist or a historian.

But I can write down what happened to me, because that's what I do. I tell stories. This one is true.

EPILOGUE

What happened to Pathology Services, PC, is not unusual; small companies go out of business all the time. The downtown streets of many communities are lined by shuttered closed businesses that once were small shops or service companies. The local general store has been replaced by Walmart. The hardware store has been replaced by Lowe's and Home Depot. The neighborhood radio/TV shop has been replaced by Best Buy.

Beyond Main Street, there has been similar consolidation. Ninety percent of the beer that consumers drink is manufactured by two companies. Air travel is dominated by only four companies. Even with a product as prosaic as shoes, one company, Nike, controls 19% of the market. My sense is that at the present time capitalism is a game that is rigged in favor of big corporations, which have the attorneys, lobbyists, accountants, and bureaucracy to keep power and tilt the game in their favor. It's get big or die. This consolidation trend has been going on for decades, and the stories of oligopoly in industry and retail are oft told. Biographies of corporate heroes like Steve Jobs, Sam Walton, Jeff Bezos, and Warren Buffet are best sellers. These corporate titans are venerated.

But this phenomenon as it relates to physician practices has been underreported, I think. I've related a few examples of replacement and consolidation of physician practices – specifically what happened to the ER docs, hospitalists, and your humble pathologist at one hospital. What happened to us is not unusual. In fact, it's common. The details change, but the results are the same – small physician groups are disappearing into large corporate structures.

This isn't a long book. I said at the outset that it's not hard to kill a small business. In my case it only took about a year for two large companies, Merciful and Excel, to kill my small company, Pathology Services. I had no choice but to sell out and become part of a larger company.

Many of my colleagues could tell a similar story. Dr. Newcombe sold his small internal medicine group with seven physicians to a large multispecialty group with several hundred physicians – with many, many internists as well as gastroenterologists, psychiatrists, allergists, endocrinologists, and otolaryngologists.

One of my best friends, a family practice doctor, sold his practice to Excel Corp. After a few years his contract was cancelled, and he was forced to retire; he was told that he didn't follow the "algorithms" and didn't meet his "metrics." It's a new world out there.

I had a recent conversation with my ophthalmologist, Dan Yates. Dan is not only my eye doctor, but he was also one of my customers; when Pathology Services was still in business, he occasionally sent specimens to us from his office practice – eyelid lesions, skin lumps and bumps around the eye, and other samples of eye maladies. Dan is a little younger than I am, and I remember when he first came to Excel Pinnacle, a young man just finishing his training who joined a thriving small ophthalmology practice with two other doctors. Dr. Yates and I worked together for a long time. Shortly after Pathology Services went out of business, it was time for my yearly eye checkup. After he finished his examination, we chatted for a little while. Dan was upset that Excel Pinnacle had fired us.

He said, "Another part of the ecosystem is gone. I don't know how much more of this kind of thing the healthcare ecosystem can take."

I said, "The lionfish have taken over the reef."

That was the last time I saw him. When it was time for my next eye exam, Dr. Dan Yates had retired and was gone for good – another loss to the ecosystem.

The details may differ, but two trends in healthcare are obvious:

1. Consolidation

2. Physicians end up as employees rather than owners

So what? Who cares if overpaid physicians lose ownership of their businesses, or even lose their jobs? Maybe no one should care.

It was probably time for me and others like me to hang it up and let the younger physicians take over as part of large healthcare institutions – insurance companies, hospital corporations, and ever-expanding academic medical centers – each with multiple billions of dollars in revenues and budgets. With such resources, these institutions with their consultants and experts can "manage society's healthcare needs" and "deliver affordable efficient compassionate patient care" using "best practices as demonstrated by quality outcomes based on standards set by expert panels." At least that's what these institutions say in their mission statements. What's wrong with that? Bigger is better, right?

Unfortunately, I contend that these two trends have not been for the better. Perhaps some of my readers think the same thing, that something important has been lost.

In 1983 when I started out in private practice, I wanted to own my own pathology practice, either by myself or with partners. After a few years, I did. I wasn't unusual. At the time more than 75% of physicians owned their own practices.

No more. By 2018 that figure was down to 46%, and that figure is dropping fast. Almost all of my colleagues are selling their practices to larger groups, or merging with other groups to form a larger group, or selling their practices to a corporation, insurance company, or academic medical center and staying on as employees. The zeitgeist is get big or die.

These changes have been very good to some, but not others. The median pay of a healthcare CEO was more than $9 million in 2020, and thirty executives made more than $30 million. The CEOs of the top six health insurance companies made a combined $236 million in 2020. But the changes have not been that good for doctors. To the contrary, between 2001 and 2020, doctors saw a 22% cut to their reimbursements. In the same time period, the costs to run a medical practice increased 39%. Those trends make it hard to stay independent. No wonder medicine is going corporate.

My observation is that this change has drawbacks in terms of patient care. With my job at an academic medical center, I spend so much time and energy navigating through the hospital's complicated bureaucratic structure and information technology system that I have little energy left to actually do my job and take care of patients.

Almost everyone I know has some horror story about a patient encounter with the healthcare system as it is today, e.g., a friend enters the hospital with nonspecific symptoms and exits a few days later to a funeral home, with no explanations from the staff to anyone – friends or family. Or a family member has a relatively minor procedure, a lymph node biopsy, and ends up with infectious complications lying in pus and blood in a bed with linen that hasn't been changed. I'm fairly certain that everyone reading this book can relate similar anecdotes.

Polls confirm this impression. Satisfaction with healthcare in this country is at an all-time low. Only 12% of patients think that healthcare in this country is handled extremely well or very well. I posit that part of the reason for this decrease in quality of healthcare, even a big part, is that large bureaucratic inflexible institutions now control medical care in America, to the detriment of both physicians and patients. For any problem that arises at a hospital, corporation, or large physician practice, its employees say the right things (as they are taught), and they are cordial and courteous (as they are trained to be), but they can't really help and actually *do* anything; they can't get that MRI done less than two weeks from now, or get that prescription filled by the pharmacy, or get that "elective" operation scheduled any time soon...because it's not their job, and in a large bureaucratic organization everyone has to stay strictly within boundaries of what they can do or are allowed to do by the billion-dollar entities now in charge of healthcare. No operation, procedure, or patient study of any cost or significance can be done without prior approval of the payer, usually an insurance company. Doctors, nurses, and technologists can only follow manuals, algorithms, policies, and procedures set forth by insurance companies, hospital corporations, experts, or other "stakeholders." They have to follow the rules, and they sure as hell better be productive – every employer has metrics to make sure of that. Creativity is not allowed. Unfortunately, I don't think such an approach works very well for taking care of patients. Each patient is different, and each patient's illness is different. Good heavens, in my practice of pathology, each specimen I receive is different, and I'm sure radiologists see an infinite variety of X-ray findings. The large entities resulting from consolidation have streamlined medical care with resultant efficiencies and decreased costs, which have increased the profits for the companies running things to the detriment of physicians. But is healthcare, actual *healthcare* better? Are patients better off? I doubt it.

ABOUT THE AUTHOR

Dr. Spenser is a practicing physician who has written several scientific articles published in various medical journals. He is also a writer. This is his fourth book.

ALSO BY JACK SPENSER, M.D.

Diary of a Malpractice Lawsuit: A Physician's Journey and Survival Guide

You Can't not Know: A Memoir about Medical School, Residency, and Life

Blood is a Special Juice

13565799R00102